TENTACLE

Rita Indiana

Translated by Achy Obejas

SHEFFIELD – LONDON – NEW YORK

This edition first published in 2018 by And Other Stories
Sheffield – London – New York
www.andotherstories.org

First published as *La mucama de Omicunlé* by Editorial Periférica in 2015
Copyright © Rita Indiana and Editorial Periférica, 2015
English-language translation © Achy Obejas, 2018

9 8 7 6 5 4 3 2 1

ISBN: 978-1-911508-34-2
eBook ISBN: 978-1-911508-35-9

Copy-editor: Lara Vergnaud; Proofreader: Sarah Terry; Typesetter: Tetragon, London; Typefaces: Linotype Neue Swift and Verlag; Cover Design: Steven Marsden. Printed and bound by CPI Group (UK) Ltd, Croydon, CRO 4YY.

A catalogue record for this book is available from the British Library.

And Other Stories gratefully acknowledge that our work is supported using public funding by Arts Council England.

For Noelia

Full fathom five thy father lies,
Of his bones are coral made;
Those are pearls that were his eyes;
Nothing of him that doth fade,
But doth suffer a sea-change
into something rich and strange.
Sea-nymphs hourly ring his knell:
Ding dong.
Hark, now I hear them.
                    Ding-dong bell.

WILLIAM SHAKESPEARE
THE TEMPEST

OLOKUN

The doorbell at Esther Escudero's house has been programmed to sound like a wave. Acilde, her maid, engaged in the day's first tasks, listens while downstairs somebody at the door of the building pushes the button to its limit and unleashes the sound over and over, canceling out the beach-like effect of the bell. Bringing her thumb and index finger together, Acilde positions her eye and activates the security camera that faces the street, where she sees one of the many Haitians who've crossed the border, fleeing from the quarantine declared on the other half of the island.

Recognizing the virus in the black man, the security mechanism in the tower releases a lethal gas and simultaneously informs the neighbors, who will now avoid the building's entrance until the automatic collectors patrolling the streets and avenues pick up the body and disintegrate it. Acilde waits until the man stops moving to disconnect and return to cleaning the windowpanes, encrusted on a daily basis with sticky soot. As she smears the windows with Windex, she sees a collector across the street hunt down another illegal, a woman who tries to hide behind a dumpster, unsuccessfully. The machine picks her up with its mechanized arm and deposits her in its main container with all the diligence of a gluttonous child picking up dirty

9

candy from the floor. A few blocks up, two other collectors work ceaselessly; from this distance Acilde cannot make out the men they're chasing. The yellow machines look like bulldozers at a construction site.

She touches her left wrist with her right thumb to activate the PriceSpy. The app tells her the brand and price of the robots in her field of vision. The brand is Zhengli, and there's a translation, *To clean up*, which appears below, next to the news and images. China's communist government donated the collectors "to help ease the terrible circumstances affecting the islands of the Caribbean after the March 19 disaster."

A flood of data blocks her vision and complicates the cleaning of the Lladró ceramics she's now turned to, so she turns off the app.

To make sure Acilde is doing her work, Esther, whose rustling at the bathroom sink can be heard in the living room, usually runs a finger somewhere in search of dust. In the old woman's collection, marine motifs predominate: fish, ships, sirens, and shells, gifts from her clients, in-laws, and terminal patients for whom the powers of Esther Escudero are a last hope. According to the media, President Bona's victory and continued power via the presidency are the work of this gray-haired woman who shuffles along in her blue silk slippers into the kitchen and pours herself a cup of the coffee Acilde has prepared for her moments before.

In her first week, Acilde broke one of these figurines, a pastel-colored pirate that pulverized when it hit the floor. Contrary to what she expected, Esther didn't scold her. "Don't touch it, something bad has left us," she said with the ceremonious gesture she used for almost every occasion. The old woman poured some water in a fig gourd and threw it all over the smashed ceramic mess. Then she gave her an order:

"Find the dustpan and broom and sweep it out to the streets through the back door." For her boss, a black butterfly meant a dark death; a burnt-out bulb, Changó needing to talk; a car alarm going off at the end of a prayer was a sign that her petition had been heard.

Before she worked at Esther's house, Acilde sucked dicks at El Mirador, without ever taking off her clothes, under which her body – with its small breasts and narrow hips – passed for that of a fifteen-year-old boy. She had a regular clientele, mostly married men, sixtyish, whose dicks only perked up in a pretty boy's mouth. She'd usually wear a polo shirt a size too big so she'd look even younger and, rather than assiduously pacing the block like her colleagues, she'd sit on a bench under an orange streetlight pretending to read a comic. The more disinterested she made her boyish self seem, the more clients she had. Sometimes she took such great pains to come off like a schoolboy out for fresh air, just leaning back on the bench, her legs crossed with a foot on her knee, that she'd forget what she was there for until a booming car horn brought her back to El Mirador and the desperate men checking her out from behind the windows of their BMWs.

This was how she'd met Eric, Esther's right-hand man, and shaken him up. A Cuban doctor with movie-star good looks, Eric didn't need to pay for sex but he was crazy about those middle-class white boys who sold themselves so they could buy the pills they were addicted to. That night in the presidential suite – what they called the patch between the bushes where the grass was softest – Acilde sucked him and let him grab her head. Eric touched her hairless cheeks and pumped them with cum, recovering his erection almost immediately. "Get naked cuz I'm gonna stick it in you," he ordered, while Acilde spit to the side, brushed off the knees

of her Levis with both hands, and asked for the five thousand pesos the blow job was worth. "I wanna screw you," Eric said, jerking off as the car lights raced over his chest and belly. Acilde hadn't quite finished saying "gimme my money, faggot" when Eric launched himself on top of her, immobilizing her, face down, and stifling her screams of "I'm a girl, shithead" with the gravel stuffed in her mouth. At this point, Eric didn't care what she was and just shoved his dry dick up her ass. When he finished and Acilde stood to pull up her pants, he flicked a lighter and approached her to confirm it was true that she was a woman. "I'm gonna pay you more for the special effects," he said. And when she saw how much more, she accepted his invitation to breakfast.

All the flimsy fried food stands the 2024 tidal wave had washed away from the Malecón reappeared in Mirador Park like flies buzzing. This new sea wall, just off a beach contaminated by unsalvageable corpses and sunken junk, felt like an oasis compared to some of the neighborhoods higher up, where the collectors pursued not only their usual targets but also the homeless, the mentally ill, and the prostitutes. She and Eric sat on plastic chairs under a colorful umbrella and ordered tostones and pork sausages. "There's nothing worse than a junkie faggot," Acilde told Eric as she swallowed the food she'd barely chewed. "They throw away their money, because mommy and daddy earn it for them, but not me. I want to study to be a chef, to cook in a fine restaurant, and save enough to get these cut off."

She was touching her breasts with both hands while Eric, now aware of their existence, thought they looked like bee stings under her T-shirt. "I can get you a better job than that, with someone who'll need you," he said.

"I don't want a husband to keep me," Acilde responded, and wiped her mouth with her sleeve.

Eric explained the deal: "It's this old santera, a friend of the president's, who needs somebody like you, young, quick, who'll cook for her and clean her house."

Acilde was perplexed. "Why would she want a dyke like me?"

Eric thought a few seconds before responding. "I can get her to pay for culinary school for you."

Acilde brought her index and middle fingers together to open her mail, then extended her ring finger, which Eric touched with his so he could see the file she wanted to share with him in his eye. It was an ad for an Italian cooking class, on sale that week, with the celebrity chef Chichi De Camps, with his chin and cashew-shaped nose, wearing an apron with his logo on it.

Acilde's room at Esther's was one of those typical rooms found in Santo Domingo's twentieth-century apartments, from when everybody had a servant who lived with them and, for a salary well below minimum wage, cleaned, cooked, washed, watched the kids, and attended to the clandestine sexual requirements of the men of the house. The explosive growth in telecommunications and factories in the Free Trade Zone had created new jobs for these women who had fled their bondage, one by one. Now, these service rooms – as they were called – were used for storage or as offices.

This job had come like a gift from heaven. Her rounds up at El Mirador had barely paid for food and data, without which she couldn't live. During her turns up there, she'd switch on the PriceSpy to check out the brands and prices of her clients' wardrobes, charging them for her services with that in mind. For her working hours, she'd prep a playlist that always ended with ABBA's "Gimme! Gimme! Gimme!" At the end of the night, she'd challenge herself to find a client, service him, and get paid before the live version of the song was over. When she did it, she'd reward herself with a plate of

four-cheese ravioli at El Cappuccino, a trattoria a few blocks from the park. She'd order in the poor Italian she'd learned online during dead time at El Mirador and imagine whole conversations with the guys who ate at El Cappuccino every day, Italians in shoes that cost more than three digits and talked about business and soccer.

In her mind, one of them, a friend of her father's, recognized the resemblance. But that was pure bullshit. Her father had stayed by her mother's side just long enough to get her pregnant. Jennifer, her mother, a brunette with good hair who'd gone to Milan with a modeling contract, had gotten hooked on heroin and ended up selling her ass on the metro in Rome. She'd had six abortions when she decided to go through with the seventh pregnancy, returning to her country so she could dump the baby on her parents, two bitter peasants from Moca who'd moved to the city after La Llorona and its two years of rain that had destroyed their homestead forever.

They beat Acilde for no reason, for being a tomboy, for wanting to play ball, for crying, for not crying. She'd compensate for the beatings at school with whoever glanced her way, and whenever she fought she'd lose track of time and a reddish light would fill her line of vision. In time, her knuckles swelled from the many scars forged from going against foreheads, noses, and walls. She had the hands of a man but that wasn't enough: she wanted the rest.

Her family detested her masculine ways. Her grandfather, César, decided to cure his granddaughter and brought over a young neighbor to see to her while he and her grandmother held her down and an aunt covered her mouth. That same night, Acilde ran away from home. She asked Peri, the class queer, if she could sleep at his place, a studio in Roberto Pastoriza, like the kind Peri's mom, Doña Bianca, rented out

to students in town. The day of the tidal wave, Acilde went down to El Mirador, along with thousands of others who were curious or who'd managed to escape still in their pajamas, to see how that terrible wave swallowed her grandparents in their smelly little apartment in the Cacique.

Peri knew entire dialogues from twentieth-century comedies no one had seen, like *Police Academy* and *The Money Pit*. In these movies, Acilde could see the easy life of fifty years ago, and it surprised her that people lived without an integrated data plan or anything. Kids from well-off homes dropped in at Peri's to take pills and, sometimes for several days in a row, to play *The Giorgio Moroder Experience*. The Sony game let you go to a 1977 disco party and dance with other "fevers," what the kids who preferred war games used to call the millions who went to the virtual party, combining the trip with pills so they could surrender to the palpitating, sensual synthesizer of Donna Summer's "I Feel Love," which lasted a whole hour. By dawn, when the pills were gone as well as the money to buy them, Peri and his friend Morla would organize a stroll to El Mirador and, after a few hours of work, they'd come back for the second half of the party.

Morla was a kid from the neighborhood. He studied law and trafficked in whatever was available: fruit trees, those drugs that were still illegal, and marine creatures, a luxury coveted by wealthy collectors now that the three disasters had finished off practically every living thing under the sea. Morla's dream was to get a government job; he lied about his background in front of Peri's other friends, children of bureaucrats who looked down on him when, using their PriceSpys, they confirmed his Versace shirts were knockoffs. It was Morla who first talked to Acilde about Rainbow Brite, an injection making the rounds in alternative science circles that promised a complete sex change without surgery. The

process had been compared to going cold turkey, although the homeless transsexuals who'd served as guinea pigs said it was much worse. In that instant, the fifteen thousand dollars needed for the drug became Acilde's only goal: she had to make that money. And since nothing better had occurred to her, that same night she went with Peri and Morla to El Mirador.

Now at Esther's, she dreamed of putting into practice what she'd learned in her cooking classes, paid for by Esther and Eric. At a restaurant in Piantini she would establish enough credit to ask for a loan and buy the wonderful vial. Her pastas drove the old woman crazy; she'd get up in the middle of the night for second helpings when she thought no one was looking. Since that terrible evening at her grandparents' house, Acilde suffered from insomnia and she'd stay up lifting weights and searching the internet for her alleged father's face. As she shaped her biceps, she'd enter the name of her progenitor into a search engine, looking for some resemblance: the wide chin or the thick eyebrows she'd inherited, which would serve her so well the day she managed to buy the drug. While searching these photos, her heart sped up, but then she'd imagine the brief email her circumstances would allow: "Hi, did you fuck a Dominican prostitute in 2008?" After her workout, she'd go to the kitchen and swallow the protein her muscles needed to grow, scaring the life out of the old woman as she ate directly out of a Tupperware container, bent in front of the freezer's open door. They'd make coffee, which they'd sip sitting together at the little kitchen table, and then Esther would tell her stories about her life and her religious vocation.

Esther Escudero was born in the seventies, during Joaquín Balaguer's twelve bloody years in power. "Almost as bloody as now," Esther would say without lifting her eyes from

her cup, ashamed of being so close to a regime the foreign press – still – did not dare call a dictatorship. "In 2004, I was thirty years old and I fell in love with my boss. I used to edit her investigative TV show on Channel 4; she was married and had a kid. Her husband wanted to kill us. I'd lived my whole life denying the things I saw and felt. It seems the husband paid for someone to put a curse on me, black magic, so I had my period nonstop. I thought I was going to die. I was already hospitalized when, one day, the woman who had been my nanny when I was a baby showed up, a woman called Bélgica, who never took off the purple handkerchief she wore on her head. She leaned down, mouth stinking of nicotine. 'We're going to Cuba,' she said. I told her she was nuts, with what money?, but she had everything ready to go. She was a poor black woman from the countryside and I couldn't understand a thing but I was so alone and so weak I let her convince me. It turns out my grandmother's family had her things and Bélgica had promised to make sure I followed in her tradition. In Matanzas I met my padrino, Belarminio Brito, Omidina, child of Yemayá, and he was so bad, as noxious as gas. But he consecrated me and returned me to life. As soon as I entered his saint's room, I stopped bleeding. Look, my hairs are standing on end. That man pulled me away from the dead souls who were trying to take me, dark souls who had been sent my way so my organs would get sick and fail. In the prophecy delivered at my initiation ceremony, it was revealed I had been cursed since I was in my mother's womb. My father's lover – a revolting bitch – had put the curses on me, and the new had joined forces with the old. These things work like that, mija, like chemistry. Omidina named me Omicunlé, after the cloak that covers the sea, because it was also prophesied that my followers would

protect the house of Yemayá. Oh, Omidina, baba mi, it's a good thing you died and didn't have to see this."

As soon as the sun came up, Esther took Acilde over to a corner of the living room and sat down on a mat on the floor. She tucked her gray mane under a pearl-colored knitted hat. She pulled a fistful of shells from a white cotton bag. With these in her hands, she began to rub the mat with circular movements. First, she asked for clarity: "Omi tuto, ona tuto, tuto ilé, tuto owo, tuto omo, tuto laroye, tuto arikú babawa." Then she celebrated all the deities that reign over the others: "Moyugba Olofin, moyugba Olodumare, moyugba Olorun . . ." She paid homage to the religion's dead: "Ibaé bayen tonú Oluwo, babalosha, iyalosha, iworó." She paid homage to her dead masters: "Ibaé bayen tonú Lucila Figueroa Oyafunké Ibaé, Mamalala Yeyewe Ibaé, Bélgica Soriano Adache Ibaé . . ." And she paid tribute to those who'd initiated her: "Kinkamanché, to my padrino Belarminio Brito Omidina, to my oyugbona Rubén Millán, Baba Latye, Kinkamanché Oluwo Pablo Torres Casellas, Oddi Sa, Kinkamanché Oluwo Oyugbona Henry Álvarez . . ." She asked Elegguá, Oggún, Ochosi, Ibeyi, Changó, Yemayá, Orisha Oko, Olokun, Inle, Oshún, Obba and Babalú Ayé, Oyá and Obbatalá for their blessing and permission to carry out the consultation. "So there will be no death, or illness, or losses, or tragedies, or arguments, or gossip, or obstacles, and so all bad things will be kept away, and we'll receive a triumphant iré, a healthy iré, an intelligent iré, a holy iré, a wedding iré, a money iré, a progressive iré, a business iré, an iré with what comes in from the sea, an iré of open roads, an iré of freedom, a work iré, an iré that goes all the way home, an iré that comes down from heaven, a balanced iré, an iré of happiness."

Of the sixteen shells she threw on the mat, four had fallen with their mouths up. "Iroso," said Esther, which was

the name of the sign on the oracle, then she lifted her face and added the sign's refrain: "Nobody knows what's at the bottom of the ocean." After throwing the shells several more times, she offered her diagnosis. "The sign is iré, which means good luck, all good. Don't cheat. Don't talk your business over with anyone, so no one knows what you're thinking or what you're going to do. Don't pass over holes or go into holes, holes in the street or holes in the countryside, because the earth will swallow you up. People like you always have jealous and hypocritical people surrounding you, as though you were a child of traps and falsehoods. You're friends with your enemy. The saint protects you from disgrace but you have to be careful and avoid prison. You'll receive inheritances and hidden riches."

Like in any good movie, Esther could make Acilde believe anything so long as she had her in front of her. As soon as she was gone, her faith would vanish too, disappearing into that world of betrayals, pacts, and dead scouts. One night, right after finishing her workout, Acilde heard a hum coming from the room where they kept the altar to Yemayá, the goddess of the sea to whom Omicunlé was devoted. Esther was sleeping. Acilde dared to go in. It smelled of incense and flower-scented water, of old fabric and the perfume of the sea held within conch shells. She approached the altar, whose centerpiece was a replica of a Greek jar some three feet tall. Eric liked to kid Esther that someday he'd inherit it; Acilde knew its exorbitant price from her PriceSpy. Depicted on the central band of the jar was an image of a woman holding a boy by the ankle as she goes to submerge him in a pool of water. All over the jar there were offerings and the attributes of the goddess: an old oar, a ship's wheel, a feathered fan. Esther had told her never to open the jar, that whoever looked inside without being initiated into the sect would go blind, or some

other crazy thing like that. But inside, perfectly illuminated and oxygenated by a mechanism adapted to the jar, Acilde saw a live sea anemone. Without putting the lid back, she looked around the bottom border of the jar to find the red eye that responded to the remote control and a small hole where a battery charger would fit perfectly. That's what the old lady was doing when she "attended" to these saints: monitoring the salt levels in the tank where she kept an illegal and very valuable specimen alive. When Acilde tried to use the PriceSpy on the animal, it just loaded endlessly. It didn't work very well with black market prices.

During the tryst that produced Acilde, her father had told her mother he wanted to get to know Dominican beaches. Back then the island was a tourist destination with coasts full of coral, fish, and anemones. She brought her right thumb to the center of her left palm to activate the camera and, flexing her index finger, she photographed the creature, then she flexed her middle finger to send the photo to Morla. She whispered a question to caption the image: "How much would they give us for this?"

Morla's response was immediate: "Enough for your Rainbow Brite."

Their plan was very simple. When the old lady left on a trip, Morla would find a way to get around the building's security, disconnect the cameras, take the anemone away in a special container, and leave Acilde tied, gagged, and free of any blame. But when Esther left for a conference on African religions in Brazil, Eric stayed in the house. At first, Acilde thought the witch didn't trust her, but later she understood the anemone needed special care, which Eric would dispense in her absence. This was confirmed when she saw him spend so many dead hours holed up in the saint's room.

On her return, Esther found Eric sick, with diarrhea, the shivers, and a strange discoloring on his arms. She sent him home.

"He asked for it, that bugger," she told Acilde. "Don't take his calls."

Despite Omicunlé's warnings, Acilde visited Eric while he was sick to bring him food and the medicine he prescribed for himself. Eric stayed in his room, where a stink of vomit and liquor reigned. There were days when he was delirious, when he sweated terrible fevers, and when he continually called out to Omicunlé: "Oló! Kun fun me lo mo, oló kun fun."

When Acilde returned to Esther's she told her everything to try to soften her up but all she managed was to get the old lady to curse him even more, calling him a traitor, dirty, a pendejo.

All the while Morla was sending Acilde desperate texts every day, trying to find out when Esther was leaving the house, when they would carry out their operation, and when, finally, he could get his hands on that anemone. Acilde had stopped answering him.

Every Thursday afternoon a helicopter would pick Esther up from the roof of the apartment building and take her to the national palace to throw the shells for the president. The consultation usually went on past midnight because the priestess would make the sacrifices and carry out the cleansings the readings recommended on the same day. These absences seemed perfect for Acilde's original plan, but recently the old lady had said and done things that had convinced her to think better of it.

Esther had brought her a blue bead necklace from Brazil; it was consecrated to Olokun, the oldest deity in the world, the sea itself.

"Master of the unknown," Esther explained when she put it on her. "Wear it always because, even if you don't believe, it will protect you. One day, you're going to inherit my house. You won't understand this now but, in time, you will."

Omicunlé would get very serious and Acilde would feel very uncomfortable. She couldn't help but feel affection for the old woman who took care of her with a tenderness her own family had never shown her. And, if she was going to let her inherit the house, couldn't she also, perhaps, give her money for the sex change?

When the doorbell's wave sounds again, Acilde is using a broom to sweep away the spiderwebs silently spun every day in the corners of the ceiling. She assumes it's another Haitian and that the security mechanism will take care of him. But then there's a knock on the apartment door. Only Eric, who has the code for the downstairs gate, could have come up. Not concerned that Esther might get mad, she runs to open the door, happy Eric is well and sure that with his cleverness he'll soon charm the priestess again.

Morla points a pistol at her. Acilde makes a move to defend herself but Morla touches her in the middle of her collarbone, pressing his fingers together to get access to her data plan's operating system. He activates both eyes, in full-screen mode, to bring up two different videos: in one eye, "Gimme! Gimme! Gimme!" and, in the other, "Don't Stop 'til You Get Enough," turning both up as loud as possible. Acilde tries to disconnect herself. Morla is too quick for her.

Blind, she screams: "Madrina, thief!" She rolls herself on the wall until she falls to the ground and feels, after a timid shot from a silenced revolver, the weight of another body falling on the marble floor.

Morla deactivates the screens. Acilde watches as he finishes off Esther. She watches him wipe off the sweat that

runs down his forehead with the back of the hand that holds the gun.

"You left me hanging, cocksucker, where is the shit?"

Now that Morla doesn't need the empathy of his little group of useless friends anymore, the killer's voice is not the same as the one he used to use at Peri's house. Acilde leads him to the saints' room and shows him the giant jar. He opens the cylinder in which he will transport his new merchandise. He's sleepless, shaking, and off his tits on coke.

"You should do another line to get yourself together," Acilde advises him.

Morla agrees, pulling out a little pink plastic bag with a piece of rock from his pocket. With a single circular motion, Acilde breaks a Lladró dolphin she's taken from the altar on his head. Morla falls to the side and the gold coins on the design of his shirt are sprinkled with blood and bits of porcelain. Acilde places the anemone in the cylinder and presses the button, activating the oxygen and the temperature the animal needs to survive.

PSYCHIC GOYA

The air conditioning was on full blast, like in all the offices in the city, so the doorknobs, desks, and toilet seats were freezing surfaces. Argenis avoided them as much as he could. Why do they turn the air up like that? Do they want to paralyze us? These were the same questions Argenis, all gooseflesh, had been asking himself for the two years he'd been working at Plusdom, a call center headquartered in an unfinished building on Independencia Avenue. The first and second floors didn't have windows or doors or floor tiles, and the stairway to the fourth didn't have a handrail. The employees climbed the stairs very carefully, staying close to the wall whenever they came back from the store with their hands full of Doritos and Cokes. Argenis worked with about twenty other Dominicans whose English was mediocre at best. He pretended to have psychic powers on a phone line that took calls from all over the United States.

He got off the toilet and pulled up his pants. He plucked a small bag of coke from his pocket. It was hard and he had to jab it a little with a key to break it up; using the same key, he sniffed a line into each nostril. He looked at himself in the medicine cabinet mirror, wiped his nose with his finger and then licked it so as not to let anything go to waste. It was only then that he flushed the toilet, never before, to make

sure nobody could calculate the time between the flush and his exit and begin to ask questions.

"That's junkie paranoia," Mirta, his ex-wife, would have said.

"I hope you drop dead," he muttered through clenched teeth as he opened the door.

The office space was divided into gray fiber cubicles. There was a desk in each cubicle, a monitor, a keyboard, and the stupid stuff people put up in those spaces to make them cozier. Diala, the pimply skinny girl who'd jerked him off once on the stairs, had hers lined with photos of REM, Morrissey, and London. Eddy, a fortyish faggot with black dyed hair, had photos of his little nieces at Disneyland. Ezequiel had pictures from his golden days: bent from the weight of three gold chains around his neck, until his mother, finding a half kilo in his closet, bought him a one-way ticket from New Jersey to his grandmother's house in Capotillo. Axel was a little white schizophrenic and this job was part of his occupational therapy; he had a stuffed Pokémon toy and posters of hyper-pop Japanese bands Argenis had never heard of. Then there was Yeyo, the moneylender, a black girl six feet tall and weighing in at two hundred pounds. He hated the fucking cunt.

Argenis sat down in his cubicle and stared at the name on the monitor he'd chosen the day he was hired: Psychic Goya. There was a call waiting. He put on his earphones and took it, his eyes fixed on the lower right corner of the screen where a clock marked how many seconds, minutes, or hours he'd managed to keep the caller on the line.

"Good evening, Psychic Goya speaking, how do you do?" he asked as a bit of bitter coke residue trickled down his throat.

It was a woman, as was almost always the case. Following Plusdom protocol, he tried to visualize her, white and horrible,

in an XXL T-shirt with some kind of promotional logo, bending her Rs and Ts with an accent from some southern backwater of the United States.

"Would you like a tarot reading today, Katherine?"

"Yes, please."

"Okay, I will pick a card for you."

There was an old tarot deck next to the monitor, which came with the desk and on which Franky, who worked the eight to four shift, would draw all sorts of obscenities with a blue Bic.

The Page of Cups was a card from the minor arcana that Argenis remembered a few things about from his two-hour training with Eddy, the veteran psychic. In the Rider-Waite deck, it was a beautiful card: an androgynous young man in a blue turban and flowered robe contemplates the fish in his cup while in the background, on the horizon, the sea tries to disguise the coming storm with an all-encompassing gray that's neither calm nor agitated. Franky had drawn several sailboats on the water and covered the page's hairless chin with a beard. On the upper left-hand corner, he'd drawn a heart traversed by a dagger bleeding straight into the cup. Argenis was surprised there weren't any hairy dicks, Franky's specialty.

Inspired by this memory, he asked, "Is your question about a young man?"

"Oh my God, you're amazing," Katherine responded.

Katherine sounded like a woman beaten down by piles of dirty dishes and a construction worker husband who showed his affection by not spitting on the rug.

Argenis dove in: "Is this man not your husband?"

Katherine screamed. "Oh my God, this is freaky."

"Psychic Goya sees all and wants to help you, Katherine. Is your husband home? No?"

Argenis talked for ten minutes straight about the card with all the eloquence his training as a visual artist allowed, threading the most typical readings of the card with whatever crap crossed his mind.

"This young man, is he an artistic fellow?"

"Yes, he likes Metallica and Marilyn Manson."

Having reached this stage, Argenis submitted her to his questionnaire about the person represented by the card until Katherine revealed everything about herself: her likes, her IQ, her house, her family, her budget. It was an exercise that burned time like hay on his computer's corner clock.

Argenis had come to Plusdom via Yeyo, the moneylender, who'd found him the job when he told her he couldn't pay back the ten thousand pesos he'd borrowed to divorce Mirta. Since then, Yeyo had controlled his life. She'd managed to get Mike, the gringo supervisor, to deduct half his salary and add it to her paycheck to help pay off his debt. "This is illegal," Argenis had complained the first time, but he gave up when he realized Mike also owed Yeyo; everybody owed Yeyo something, money or favors, and she knew how to extract interest. Argenis paid off the debt in seven months but almost immediately took out another loan so he could buy coke from Ezequiel, who had gotten back into his old business as soon as he'd landed in Santo Domingo. Argenis began buying half a gram on Wednesdays, because Thursday was his day off, and later, with the excuse of the night shift and the divorce, he justified a gram a day, which made him fall behind on the electric bill, the only one his mother had asked him to help with when he moved back in with her.

Yeyo was cousins with one of Argenis' classmates at the School of Fine Arts, where he'd graduated in 1997. Back then, she'd helped with a few of his financial difficulties – money to buy materials, Fabriano paper, oil, and canvas – nothing

he couldn't pay back right away since his father, who worked for the governing party, would send him a monthly allowance Argenis used to pay rent on a studio facing Colón Park, where he'd pick up lost foreign girls who showed up in the Colonial Zone, drunk on Brugal, Haitian pot, and Guns N' Roses.

It was there that Argenis would daydream about his future as a visual artist. His talent was unquestionable. He'd won dozens of drawing contests as a child and his professors back in the seventies used to invite him to sit with them in the cafeteria. At the School of Fine Arts, a public institution with a budget even smaller than the local barbershop's, the professors – for whom there was no art after Picasso – were proud of Argenis' technical expertise and Catholic themes and predicted a successful and prosperous future for him.

But when he finished at the School of Fine Arts and got his father to send him to the School of Design at Altos de Chavón, it was a different story. His fluency with perspective and proportion wasn't worth a dime. His classmates were rich kids with Macs and digital cameras who talked about Fluxus, video art, video action, and contemporary art. They had Hello Kitty backpacks and talked in English and French; it was impossible to tell if they were queer.

The first week, the new students put on a slide show to show their portfolios. When he saw their collages, photos, and little drawings, Argenis grew haughty at the thought of how much he was going to teach these ignoramuses. He was sure his Renaissance virgins and archangels would dazzle them; he'd used working-class German, Swiss, and Spanish tourists as models for them in his Colonial Zone studio. The next day, during the first art history class, Professor Herman decided to begin with what had happened in the last ten years, the nineties. Marina Abramović, Jeff Koons, Takashi Murakami, Santiago Sierra, Damien Hirst, Pipilotti Rist. She

explained everything very well, including the price of the works and each artist's references. Argenis' blood sugar tanked. He had to excuse himself, walking with blurry eyes to the mini-mart. Where the hell had he been? He felt poor, ignorant, and, above all else, confused. The works he had seen, even if sometimes they'd been made not by the artist but by a toy factory in China, belonged in form and vitality to their time, just as the works of Velázquez and Goya had belonged to theirs. He remembered the squalid cafeteria where he'd spent hours as an alienated young man, listening to painters with black teeth share the secrets of Leonardo, Rembrandt, and Dürer. What utter bullshit.

Altos de Chavón was a replica of a Mediterranean village from the sixteenth century. A millionaire came up with the idea when his highway project ran into a stone mountain. Charles Bluhdorn, the president of Gulf+Western, and his friend Roberto Coppa, a set designer for Paramount, built the place with the very stones that, for other men, might have been an obstacle. The idea for a school of art and design came as soon as the town was completed; it would be the only alternative on the island to the pathetic School of Fine Arts.

A month after arriving, Argenis had not made a single friend and was envious of the parties in the dorms the kids from the Lycée Français and Carol Morgan would throw. The parties would wind up at the pool or the beaches in Bayahibe, where the kids would drive in their brand-new Alfa Romeos. With his studio door open, just in case anybody wanted to ask him to join in, he'd pretend to read *The Shock of the New*, which he'd borrowed from the library. When he finally gave up, he'd walk aimlessly around the faux structures, which could offer no history for that fake medieval village.

One of those nights Argenis emptied a bottle of Brugal Añejo by himself and was wandering around the school

until, without realizing it, he ended up in a small patch of bougainvillea. Thorns spanning half a hand in length scratched his face and arms. The full moon snuck through the creeper's manic shadows, as did the voices of a group of students who saw him from outside and tried to contain their laughter. When he couldn't find his way out, he threw himself on the ground, whimpering in a puddle of vomit until he fell asleep. From the depths of that disgusting dizziness, he heard a woman's voice. She called to him: "Goya, Goya," and he thought: My prayers have been answered and I've woken from my nightmare as Goya.

He opened his eyes and saw Professor Herman, wearing a pink Nike jacket for her early morning jog, kneeling next to him. The first rays of sunlight drenched her face, half Moorish and half Inca, in orange. She'd crossed the tangle of thorns to help him. "Goya, get up." He sat and saw the dried bloody scratches on his arms and smelled the dry vomit, and he felt shame and, then, more shame when he learned that that was what everyone at school called him, Goya, because they didn't recognize his insecurities and thought he was full of shit. Professor Herman explained all this to him in her apartment, where she'd taken him so the others wouldn't see him come back to the dorm in his condition. She let him take a shower, lent him a pair of shorts and a T-shirt, and put hydrogen peroxide and mercurochrome on his wounds. Later, she made him a cup of black coffee so he could take two aspirins and she stacked a pile of books on the table: *The Aesthetics of Disappearance, Society of the Spectacle, Mythologies, The Kingdom of This World, The Invention of Morel*, and *Naked Lunch*. He hadn't said a word. She yanked on his dreadlocks and said, "Wake up, Goya, get it together. You have impeccable technique but nothing to say. Look around, damn it, do you think a bunch of little angels is what's needed here??"

Professor Herman managed to get him excused from the anatomical drawing classes, which Argenis didn't need, so he could study what she assigned to him: mostly books and films. By the end of the first year, Goya had made a couple of friends he'd lured in with the Haitian marijuana he copped in the city, and though his work still looked like illustrations by a Jehovah's Witness, they now had a certain irony.

What would Professor Herman say if she saw him now? In a fucking call center, fucking "Psychic Goya," with a goddamned fat ass charging him ten percent on each peso he borrowed, with not a single exhibition to his name since graduation – divorced, bitter, and aimless. He heard the woman's voice on the other end of the line: "Goya, Goya, are you there?" And then he felt the cold shock of an ice cube somebody had slipped down his sweater as it rolled down the crack of his ass and soaked his butt cheeks. He turned to kill the son of a bitch and found Yeyo, a Burger King cup in her hand, choking from laughter along with Diala and Ezequiel. With one hard slap, he knocked the drink out of her hand, sending it flying along with the cup. "I've had it with you, you fucking nigger!" he heard himself exclaim. Yeyo's eyes watered and she marched straight to Mike's office. Fifteen minutes later, Mike came out hugging Yeyo with one arm and holding out Argenis' last check with the other.

Etelvina Durán, a Spanish professor at the Autonomous University, was a strong light-skinned woman, the daughter of peasants from La Vega, who had been a militant with various leftist movements since she was sixteen. She'd met Argenis' father at a meeting of the Communist Party of the Dominican Republic. They had seen half their friends killed by Balaguer's assassins. Their own lives had been spared because Etelvina's brother, a Marine lieutenant, had pulled them out from in front of a firing squad in Ensanche Ozama one early

morning in 1975 when he recognized Etelvina among the hotheads he was supposed to execute. At dawn, José Alfredo, the slim leftist who did the best impression of Johnny Ventura, married her, left his life in hiding, and joined the ranks of the recently established Party for Dominican Liberation, to which he remained faithful, selling newspapers for the two decades it took for them to come to power. Etelvina had supported José Alfredo so he could dedicate all his time to the party. She'd managed by sewing, studying, and raising Argenis and his older brother, Ernesto, until José Alfredo left her for a fellow member of the party, who had agreed to pay for him to go to law school in Pucamaima. Etelvina had not been with a man since. She had devoted herself to her sons and her work. She'd stayed close to her leftist friends, watching as they settled, like her, into inoffensive lives as dentists, insurance salesmen, and veterinarians who got together on Saturdays to sing songs by Silvio at karaoke. Ernesto had proven outstanding at school and sports, winning a scholarship to study political science in Argentina while Argenis had smoked pot, listened to Alpha Blondy cassettes, and grown dreadlocks, which his father never forgave him for. Etelvina loved it whenever José would look at the dreads with disgust; she supported her son, forcing his father to pay for his studies and send him a monthly allowance. Back then Argenis was her treasure. In his rebelliousness and artistic talent she saw a harmless reflection of her own protest days and her secret desire to write poetry. She'd kept a little notebook since the seventies in which she'd written free verse, and she still returned to it on special occasions. No one knew about this. The notebook, yellowed now, sat next to a Roque Dalton anthology on the one bookshelf in the house. These days, her expectations of Argenis had also yellowed.

As soon as he'd finished at Altos de Chavón, Argenis had married a girl who worked at a bank. She was a woman with an incredible body who'd read everything she could and chosen to study business so she didn't have to hustle. She'd used her salary as an assistant manager to support Argenis for an entire year while he supposedly put together his first solo show. Then, one day, she'd packed his stuff into three suitcases and taken them over to Etelvina's. "Your son is worthless," she said. "He spends all day doing coke and watching porn on his computer while I'm working my ass off nine to five." Argenis showed up at his mother's apartment two days later with stitches on his brow because, when he'd refused to leave the apartment, Mirta had smashed a bottle on his head and told him she was two months pregnant but was getting rid of the shitty little creature inside her that very afternoon.

What hurt Argenis most was the abortion and he fell into a deep depression in his childhood bedroom, which Etelvina had turned into a sewing room. She filled him up with sedatives she bought without a prescription from a pharmacist friend so she wouldn't have to listen to him crying and slurping snot. A month after the divorce, she got him out of bed with a bucket of cold water. One week later, Argenis was at Plusdom and every morning, when he came home from work, he'd bring her a fresh loaf of bread and a Tetra Pak of milk. She could not figure out how he'd managed to get himself fired from such an idiotic job, and when he got home, still coming down from the coke and weak and tired, to tell her he was jobless again, she didn't let him sleep until almost midnight, yelling at him that he was a "layabout, sad sack, August turd," among other insults, each one a gem from the Cibao region.

At six the following morning, she got him up so he could make her breakfast, clean the house, and wash the car. "I'm

not gonna continue to be a sucker supporting a grown man, goddamn it." Argenis made her some toast and scrambled eggs but she bitched about the texture of the eggs as she chewed open-mouthed. The egg spittle flying in the air let Argenis know he'd lost the only thing he'd had left in the world.

At about ten, he rolled up his trousers and went down to the garage with a bucket, a hose, and a sponge to wash the green Toyota Corolla his mother had managed to buy only recently, after having raised them exclusively on public transportation. When the party came to power in 1996, José Alfredo had begun working as an advisor to the president and had signed over a check for one hundred and fifty thousand pesos to Etelvina to make up for the little he'd contributed in support while the boys were growing up. She wasn't interested in finding out how her ex-husband had gotten his hands on such a large sum of money and bought herself a car that, to date, she had not once lent to her son. Argenis connected the hose to the faucet, poured some water on his head and face, and then turned it on the Toyota to dissolve the hardened dirt. He stuck the soapy sponge in the bucket and saw himself reflected in a window: unshaven, cheeks prominent, a scar on his brow, and the dreadlocks, which, thanks to his sudden hair loss, looked like strings of cat turds. His mother was up on the apartment's balcony, supervising him as though he were not even capable of washing a car.

On the other side of the street, a brand-new Montero slid into a parking space and a man emerged with his hair combed back like Robert De Niro in *The Godfather Part II*, wearing a blue linen shirt, khaki Bermuda shorts, and canvas sandals. Giorgio Menicucci looked more like he was about to get on a catamaran than run around the streets of Santo Domingo. He didn't wait to close the door of the Montero before he checked himself in the window, like Argenis had just done,

fixing his hair with his hand though it didn't need it, and adjusted his pants, which he'd cinched with a braided leather belt. As he crossed the street, he recognized the car washer and smiled and picked up his pace.

Argenis knew Giorgio from the cultural activities sponsored by the Chavón Foundation, which he attended with his wife, Linda Goldman, the daughter of Jewish refugees to whom Trujillo had given lands in 1939 in the town of Sosúa, on the northern coast. Linda was the most beautiful thing Argenis had ever seen in his life. She had perfect tits, which would fill but not overflow his hands, alert green eyes that suggested she'd never done one stupid thing in her life, and almond hair. She gathered her locks in a bun, which showed off her ears and gave advance notice of her other deliciously sweet holes. Argenis knew they had bought work from other students for their Caribbean art collection and threw parties that lasted three days at their private beach in Sosúa.

For both these reasons he'd approached them during an opening at the Chavón Archaeology Museum, back when he still had enough self-esteem to do that kind of thing. Argenis had found them admiring a Taino pot; the heart-shaped piece with a phallic growth emerging between two breasts was the inspiration for a lot of jokes at school. Argenis had known to keep that kind of childish humor in check. "A very sophisticated notion of sexuality, no?" he'd said, repeating one of Professor Herman's phrases. "I would have made a bigger penis," Giorgio said, which made his wife laugh aloud. Nonetheless, they showed interest in him. They were charming and straightforward, because people with money don't have to engage in the usual bullshit to rise above others. After the opening, Argenis invited them to his studio and, after sacrificing his last joint, he showed them what he'd been painting now that Altos de Chavón had saved him from becoming

an illustrator for catechism books. He explained that he still believed in painting, even though others dismissed the discipline as though it were macramé. He was working on a large-format piece: deep in a forest of thorns, and recasting the roles from Michelangelo's *Pietà*, a nude man read a comic in the lap of a woman wearing a Nike jacket with a sky-blue hood. Up close, you could see the comic's cover: *New Gods 1* by Jack Kirby, from 1971. Giorgio was more impressed with Argenis' technique than the costumes he had assigned the figures in the proposed piece, and he commissioned a portrait of him, Linda, and their dog, a Weimaraner called Billy.

The portrait was the last piece Argenis had sold. Now he regretted having just given Giorgio the pencil studies he'd done before completing the forty-eight-by-seventy-inch painting in which the Menicuccis appeared with hair-raising exactitude on their terrace facing the sea. Linda sat on a grand wicker sofa with her foot on top of Billy, who was on his back for her to rub his belly, while Giorgio stood, wearing only swim trunks, and challenged the spectator with both his fists out front like a boxer. A Wifredo Lam painting they'd received as a wedding present hung on the back wall. It featured a black and red thorny figure that Argenis had reproduced with rough brushstrokes. Everything was drenched in the light of a late afternoon in which the limits of the flesh dissolved into white and yellow particles in the same way life itself appears to dissolve under a microscope. If I had those studies now, I could sell them to him, Argenis thought, as Giorgio, smelling of Issey Miyake, hugged and greeted him in Italian, like he did his dog.

"I've come to make you an offer you can't refuse," said Giorgio, putting a hand on his shoulder. His hand was warm and soft but, for Argenis, any kind of physical closeness with another man made him break out in hives. He used turning

off the hose as an excuse to get out from under the uncomfortable contact. Giorgio kept talking. He'd come to invite
him to participate in a project; he'd get room and board for
six months and the assistance of a Cuban curator. The Sosúa
Project, as Giorgio called it, was a cultural, artistic, and social
endeavor that he hoped would give something back to the
country that had made him rich.

What Argenis knew about Giorgio's past was what
Professor Herman, a friend of the Menicuccis, had told him.
He'd arrived in 1991, an Italian from Switzerland, without
a dime to his name. His talents had helped him get a job as
a chef in the kitchen of an all-inclusive hotel called Playa
Dorada. Soon he had his own artisanal pizzeria in Cabarete,
the Caribbean capital of water sports, where he'd met Linda,
back then a rich girl windsurfing champion who offered
lessons to tourists on the beach. She was going through an
I-hate-being-rich phase and supported herself with what she
earned from the lessons. Her father, Saul Goldman, who'd
arrived on the island as a young boy fleeing concentration
camps and had made his fortune from scratch with a dairy,
found her attitude heartwarming and talked about his independent daughter with a wink. Years before, he'd seen her
go off to study marine biology at Duke University and had
asked God to put a Jewish boy in her path. But Linda found
gringos insipid and came home with the idea of starting a
foundation to protect the coral reefs in Sosúa and, later, the
entire island. Her father said no, that it would mean risking
the livelihoods of the local fishermen, who had families
just like he did. Linda tried to explain, in a language that
was perhaps too scientific, that we were headed toward the
complete extermination of all our marine life. "Extermination
is a strong word, you shouldn't use it when talking about
animals," the old man said.

With what he made at the pizzeria, Giorgio had been saving to buy a slice of the beach at Sosúa, a strip of sand at the foot of a cliff called Playa Bo that he'd become obsessed with. Giorgio let Linda keep the surfboards she gave her lessons with in the alley by his restaurant – neighborly camaraderie – until the day he took her to the little beach of his dreams to impress her with a corner of the town that even she, who'd been born there, didn't know existed. As they made their way down from the indented cliff to the sand, they saw an enormous school of surgeonfish, an electric-blue stream shooting out of a hole in the coral reef that framed the beach. Giorgio told her that when he'd first arrived, he used to sleep in the little shanty the peasant owners had built there. Later he explained that he wanted to buy the place to make it a sanctuary, free of fishing and other pillaging. They were both up to their necks in the water and he had started to float on his back with his eyes closed, very close to her, relaxed and beautiful, like a dolphin with his wet and nearly hairless skin. She didn't wait for him to sit up. "You're going to marry me," she said, "and we're going to buy this beach."

The Playa Bo Argenis saw in 2001 had gone through a process of eco-friendly construction. Where before there had been a forest of brambles and guasábaras, there was now a modern one-story concrete and wood house, with an enormous brick terrace that looked out at the sea. The cliff and the beach were to the left of the house, where they had built a wooden staircase for better access to the water. The exterior walls were glass and the interior walls were wooden modules the owners moved around according to their needs and that of their guests. The kitchen and the bathrooms were the only permanent rooms; the constant coming and going of art, appliances, and furniture kept everything "in process," as Linda liked to say. Argenis – who knew the house

from photos he'd been given to help him render the family portrait – and the other members of the Sosúa Project weren't regular guests and instead took up residence for the duration of the project in some cabins, recently built for them, a few meters from the house. The studios would serve as both workspaces and shelter; they were well-lit and breezy, each with a bed, a couch, a worktable, a TV, and a ceiling fan, all painted white and devoid of decor. Giorgio took Argenis to his, though he hadn't signed the contract yet because he wanted to see the lodgings for himself.

According to the contract, Giorgio and Linda, or, actually, their gallery, Menicucci / Contemporary Art, would keep forty percent of the art sold by the artists, who would be represented exclusively by the gallery. Giorgio opened the studio curtains so the morning light could come in through the window. When he saw the space, Argenis felt ashamed at not having signed earlier and feared Giorgio would retaliate by sending him back to the city on the midday bus. Billy, who always trailed after his master, sniffed the corners of the studio before doing the same to Argenis, who feigned a quick pat of the dog and quickly signed with the A and L he used to mark his paintings. Just then a huge guy, black as coal, came into the studio. He was wearing cutoff jeans, a Dodgers cap, and a Tommy Hilfiger polo with a faded collar. His belly was hard and prominent, although his arms and legs had the muscle definition of an ex-athlete. He and Giorgio hugged like little girls. "Maestro," Giorgio said to Argenis with a deference he really wanted to sound sincere, "this is the next global star of performance art, Malagueta Walcott, another of our artists." Contact between two men, and so near to him, always made Argenis uncomfortable. "Can we go down to the beach?" he asked, wanting to get away from the proximity of the bed.

Up to her waist in the still pool the reef formed at Playa Bo, Linda was filling test tubes while another gringo introduced what looked like a thermometer into the water. "James is an oceanographer from UCLA. They're running tests because we want to turn Playa Bo into a sanctuary," Giorgio explained. "We have to protect the sea or . . ." he said, making a gun with his hand and pointing it at Argenis' head before shooting. Argenis could not give three fucks about their environmentalist passions. But Linda, in her wetsuit, struck him as the best part of the project. He imagined jerking off between her breasts while Giorgio talked about coral species. He had to recall the ice cube Yeyo had put down his back to avoid an erection.

That night, around the teak table on the big terrace, Argenis met the other participants, Elizabeth Méndez and Iván de la Barra. She was a video artist who'd gone to school with him at Altos de Chavón and had never once said a word to him. Iván de la Barra was a Cuban curator, a "critical piece of the experiment," according to Giorgio's introduction, which he gave as he served a finger's worth of Bordeaux in his cup. Iván tasted the wine and nodded, playing as though he were a customer at a restaurant and Giorgio was the waiter. They both laughed when Giorgio finished filling the cup, which Iván turned to one side, spilling a few drops on the ground to satisfy the thirst of the dead and to ask for "material and spiritual development for the neophytes." Malagueta pulled out a notebook and asked for the meaning of "neophyte." Argenis was embarrassed for him. Iván explained: "A neophyte is a novice, a person who's just integrated into the community. You're a neophyte."

In spite of the sweet sea breeze, the quarter moon hovering over the horizon, Giorgio's pesto, and the curator's enviable talent at holding forth on history, philosophy, and popular

culture, Argenis could feel a sour gas rising in his esophagus: Fucking Cubans, now this cocksucker is going to come here to show us how to A-E-I-O-U? And this damned nigger, so stupid with his little notebook, he couldn't just look up the word in a dictionary? Everybody loves them because of their goddamned revolution but how long is that good for? You only have to be Cuban to get invited to Spain, to Japan. What's this layabout going to show me? I mean, people back in Cuba give their asses for a tube of toothpaste. There he goes: blah blah architecture, blah blah film. I don't care, here we got salami with rice and beans. Go wipe your own butt, you cocksucker . . .

The next day, Iván detailed the program for them on the second floor of Argenis' loft. It had a digital projector, several armchairs, and a blackboard on which the Cuban had just written the word PINAKOTHIKI. Everyone had brought a notebook except Argenis. "While we're here, we're going to learn that the creative process is art in itself, and along the way we're going to question the shape and content of our work." Iván talked as he walked between the armchairs, like a professor. He was a slender man, with an aquiline nose, deep waves in his hair, and youthful acne. He loved to savor his Cuban accent, using it to charm his audience into accepting everything he was saying. He wasn't wrong often. And he had a wicked sense of humor. "Mr. Luna, why do you want to be an artist?" Iván didn't wait for Argenis to answer and was already off again, now pontificating about the instinct to preserve art and the artist's instinct to preserve an idea in time, to manifest a mental image, a sensation, a philosophical conclusion. But Argenis wasn't listening anymore, because the question had stirred thoughts of his father, who, now that the party had lost, was living off what he had been able to accumulate during four years in power and preparing

little skirmishes so they could win the next elections. Argenis had been lucky to get Giorgio's invitation. Jobless and with his father out of the Palace, he wasn't going anywhere. He looked over at Elizabeth, who had a good ass and little tits with big nipples you could see through her braless T-shirt. He entertained himself by imagining Malagueta sticking it to her on Iván's desk, with his balls, which must have been blue, swaying to the rhythm.

At noon they had lunch out on the terrace. Argenis thought if they were going to eat together every day he would have to put a bullet in his brain. And then Linda asked if they wanted to go snorkeling later that afternoon. "It's beautiful, there are so many fish, and it's super relaxing, isn't it?" she asked Billy, who barked in response. "What do you say?" she asked Argenis directly. Instead of taking the gesture as a friendly invitation to try and bring a melancholy and distant character into the group, Argenis began to put things together: She's mine! She's not gonna give it away to the nigger and Iván must be a faggot. She wants me to fuck her.

During dessert, the Cuban kept eyeing Elizabeth's CD rack, which was full of dance music – Daft Punk, Miss Kittin, Cassius. That's how Giorgio had met her: Elizabeth went to all the parties in the city, in abandoned basements and hotel discotheques that hadn't changed since the sixties. The crowd was small and diverse, and people came for the music and the ecstasy. Argenis had never been to one and never popped a tuerca, as Giorgio very naturally referred to pills, and all he could imagine was a provincial atmosphere, like the discos his female friends went to in high school to dance merengue and look for boyfriends.

At the beach, Linda distributed wetsuits and snorkels, dove in first, and signaled for them to follow her along the coral reef that enclosed the row of dogteeth encircling the

pool at Playa Bo. They swam their way around schools of mackerel until they reached a giant rock with a hole about three feet in diameter and a tunnel of blue light from which emerged a little group of damselfish and a parrotfish. Argenis thought everything was very beautiful, but he wanted to see Linda's pussy and Malagueta's big head was always in the way. Linda went through the hole in the rock and the rest of them waited for her to come back. Hesitating, Argenis saw his chance and went after her. It took all of them to bring him back to the surface, vomiting water and with anemone stings and scratches everywhere. "He didn't get very far," said Malagueta, "and he's, like, burnt on his back." He was laughing nervously, a hand over his mouth as he recalled how Argenis had spazzed as soon as he went in the hole. "Like a fish on a hook," said Elizabeth. "Shit, man. What a bad trip."

CONDYLACTIS GIGANTEA

When she left Esther's house, Acilde had avoided official taxis and the metro, where cameras would follow her, and taken a ride in a public car. These old jalopies – Japanese models from the early years of the century – were still on the streets in spite of government efforts to pull them from circulation. Their reasonable price and privacy made them ideal for fugitives and the undocumented. The drivers knew the alleys up in the high part of the city and would detour from their routes for a bit more money. Villa Mella, where she'd asked the driver to take her, was the cradle of the evangelical terrorist movement that had emerged after President Bona had declared the 21 Divisions, with its blend of African deities and Catholic saints, as the official religion. The Servants of the Apocalypse, as the enemies of all that was not biblical called themselves, liked to place explosives and kill people almost as much as speaking in tongues. Acilde figured the police wouldn't take long to finger her and that she'd only find refuge for a few days among those who thought Esther Escudero was an object of demonic adoration and deserved to die.

In the Kemuel commune, an assembly praised God's name with loudspeakers and encouraged believers to help bring about Armageddon on the island. Acilde bet they'd probably

already seen her on the Web, where her photo would have been shown next to Morla's, and blamed her for the crime. She approached two girls wearing tangled braids and floor-length skirts and asked to be taken to one of their leaders. Melquesidec, a pastor with sausage-like fingers, had an office nearby with a desk, two folding chairs, and some faded and stained cushions on a bed of newspapers, from when they still used to print on paper, that was serving as a couch. On the wall, hanging off a single nail, there was a belt with a mountain knife. Next to it, a poster read: "And the angel threw his sickle to earth, and harvested the vine of the earth, and threw the grapes into the great winepress of God's anger."

Melquesidec ordered her to sit. Lies, thought Acilde, are like beans, they have to be well seasoned or no one will swallow them. She made up a dream with a lamb on an altar whose blood formed the letters of Esther Escudero's name. She added things she remembered from the Sunday school her aunt had made her attend as a child. The minister who'd taught those classes oozed the same social resentment as Melquesidec; his dealings with girls of twelve and thirteen had put a price on his head. Melquesidec fixed his reddened eyes on Acilde with an otherworldly lust that made her feel more sorry for him than for her clients at El Mirador. "Little sister, the Lord has anointed you and I must protect his work," he said, scratching a nipple with the nail of his pinky. He ordered Brother Sofonías, a young man with a mild case of Down syndrome, to make her feel at home. Before Acilde could stand, Melquesidec had stuck a spit-covered finger in her ear.

Sofonías was very tall, and his tiny eyes were shiny with a false happiness; like everyone else in that place, he smelled like a dirty toilet. The commune took up several blocks, with improvised housing made of wood, zinc, and, sometimes, cement. They had irregular water and electricity, just like

in all the neighborhoods outside the central circuit, where not even the collectors bothered to come. He took her by the arm to a one-room shanty with a dirt floor and pushed her inside. He closed the three-plank door and locked it from the outside. She heard him drag a plastic chair over to the front of the door and drop into it with a deep sigh. Inside, alone, Acilde looked around without taking off her backpack, in which she was carrying the anemone. The room would have been perfect for keeping a dog or a frightened woman. Acilde tested a plank of plywood at the back of the room and without needing to be kicked twice, the rotted wood fell apart, creating a hole she could escape through without too much noise. All the while, Sofonías sang: "To the battle march with firm conviction/ behind Christ, our Captain/ our hearts swollen with manly ardor/ to defeat Satan's army."

Leaping over streams of black water, she ran away from the fanatics' commune until she reached an avenue where a group of little kids was selling crack to the cars lined up to buy. She went up to the youngest in the group and, using money as bait, got him to take her home with him. He lived with his pregnant sister, who was sitting in front of a pedestal fan eating a plate of rice and salami when they arrived. "I'm not gonna fuck anybody, Joel, I'm eating," Samantha said, hitting the plate with her fork. Without mentioning the bills in his pocket, Joel stuck his hand in her plate and grabbed a piece of sausage. "Just looking for a place to crash," he said.

Acilde saw there was a tablet on a little table in the middle of the room. As soon as she'd left Esther's house, she'd disconnected her data plan so she couldn't be located, but now she needed to reach Eric, the only person who could help her. The tablet was an old model that ran on an independent plan only offered on the city's periphery. Samantha made

a move to grab it back but Acilde explained, typing on the screen, that she only needed it for a few minutes. "What, now we're a five-star hotel, asshole?" asked the girl as she disappeared with a plate of plantains behind the little curtain that separated the kitchen and the sitting room. Joel showed Acilde the only bedroom, which had a twin bed. "And your sister?" Acilde whispered, busy with the tablet. But Joel was already in the kitchen, serving himself whatever had been left on the stove.

Acilde sent Eric a picture of a monkey. Eric sent back a photo of the Titanic. Acilde responded with a photo of the Titanic at the bottom of the sea and a photo of a rainbow. After a minute of more photos, Acilde had sent him one of Pancho Villa, one of Matías Mella, another of Mama Tingó, and one of a postcard of a sunset on the beach from back when the sea reflected the sky and wasn't just contaminated chocolate. The monkey was still the most well-known call for help. Even the police knew what it meant. Eric got the message: Acilde was in Villa Mella, in deeper than the Titanic, she had the sea creature with her, and she would return it to him in exchange for Rainbow Brite. She'd wait for him around the Mama Tingó metro station after dark.

Eric had taken care to come in a public car, a 2007 Honda Civic, which still preserved the original ash gray paint job twenty years later. The Cuban climbed out of the car and pulled a suitcase from the trunk. He looked wasted and shaky and Acilde rushed to help him with the luggage. She brought him up to date as they strolled through the plastic garbage-laden puddles on the way to Joel's. Once there, Eric gave Samantha two hundred dollars and ordered her and Joel to leave. "Go find someplace else to stay for a few days. You won't want to be here when the cops come."

"I didn't kill her," Acilde said as soon as they were alone.

"That's not important now. I'm going to help you with the shot. You can't do it yourself."

Acilde was surprised by this reaction; maybe his illness had finally done him in. He pulled out five IVs, gauze and clamps, several bottles, and a piece of cascarilla Esther had used to trace white lines on doors and in the corners of her apartment.

He ordered Acilde to give herself an enema, take a bath, and shave her vulva and head. She did everything with a little shaver, thinking all the while: This guy's a doctor, he knows what he's doing. He made her lie down on the bed, over which he'd erected a kind of white tent to keep the space around her body sterile. There was a plate of uncooked rice at the foot of the bed. "You're getting pretty folkloric," Acilde said, anxiously watching as Eric pulled a sealed metallic envelope out of a jacket pocket. He tore the envelope with his teeth. "They're offerings so everything will go smoothly," he explained, showing her a vial with about two inches of a white and viscous liquid in it. "It'd better work, cuz it cost me my right ball," he said as he filled a syringe that danced in his hand. When he showed Acilde some latex belts, she sprang up from the bed. "I'm just following instructions," he said and cackled like a chicken to test her courage. Defiantly, Acilde lay back down and let him tie her with the belts. "Try to break loose," he said. She struggled but couldn't move.

Before beginning, Eric took a quick look at the jar where the sea anemone rested. It was in bad shape, like him, and he'd have to act fast. As soon as the Rainbow Brite entered her bloodstream, Acilde began to convulse. I've killed her, thought Eric. They sold me rat poison! But she soon stabilized and he checked her vital signs at intervals. Two hours later she complained about the heat and later still told him she was burning alive. When the bed began to shake from

her tremors, Eric gave her a sedative. At midnight her small breasts began to fill with smoky bubbles as her mammary glands consumed themselves, leaving a wrinkled web that looked like gum around her nipple, which Eric removed with pincers so it wouldn't get infected. Underneath grew a masculine skin. Her cells reconfigured themselves like worker bees around her jaw, her pectorals, her neck, her forearms, and her back, filling up to become hard where before there were just soft curves. It was daybreak when the body, confronted with the total annihilation of the female reproductive system, convulsed again. With contractions that made her lower abdomen rise and fall, she expelled what had been her uterus through her vagina. Her labia sealed in a cellular fizz and quickly formed a scrotum, which would give birth to the testicles, while her clitoris grew, making her stretching skin bleed. Eric removed the old skin as he had done around her nipples, sterilizing as he went along, as the makers of Rainbow Brite advised. At noon the next day, Acilde Figueroa was wholly a man. Eric protected his designer body, still encased in raw flesh, with layers of anti-septics and cotton.

Eric sat in a plastic chair next to the bed and battled sleep by contemplating his own death. He thought the scene where death would find him was amusing, and this, his last act of caring for a patient, seemed straight out of the mission statement of the Latin American School of Medicine in Cuba, where he'd graduated. "Science and conscience" was the mantra at the school, which had been founded to create an army of white-robed doctors in service to the most needy, and whose Third World missions the Castros used to excuse everything that had gone wrong with the revolution.

At sunset the Servants of the Apocalypse screamed verses into loudspeakers that the wind blew right into the room:

"He had seven stars in his hand, and from his mouth emerged a sharp double-bladed sword." Eric was astonished as he watched the powerful drug accelerate the healing process. The metamorphosis was reaching its conclusion: the skin that would forever protect this masterpiece now covered every altered centimeter of flesh. In contrast to this body's robust health, Eric's was deteriorating. His fragile lungs, already filled with liquid, began to hurt more than he could bear. He'd made a mistake, but at least he was on the verge of finishing the job for which he'd been put on earth.

Eric was nine years old when, playing marbles one afternoon in the hallway of his home, his eyes rolled back when he tried to look at his mother, as if he were having an epileptic fit, and he shot out of the house.

They found him on the outskirts of the city, at a ritual in honor of Yemayá, where he'd come by himself, speaking in tongues, speaking in Yoruba. That same year, Omidina, who was also Esther Escudero's godfather, initiated Eric as Babalosha.

In the prophecy delivered at his initiation, it was revealed he would be the one to find Olokun's legitimate son, the one with the seven perfections, the Lord of the Deep. That's why his godfather called him Omioloyu, the Eyes of Yemayá, convinced that one day this clever young boy would discover in the flesh the one who knew what lies at the bottom of the sea.

The oracle had told Esther Escudero, Omicunlé, that she would receive the Chosen One in her own home, and that she would meet her death at his hands. She'd accepted that future calamity with equanimity. She trusted Eric to carry out her plan to have him initiate Omo Olokun when she was no longer here. Eric loved the old woman like a mother and, wanting to avoid the prophecy's fatal outcome, he'd tried to improvise a way out. If he crowned himself as Omo Olokun,

he could get rid of Acilde, the supposed Chosen One, but his experiments with the anemone behind Esther's back had ended up making him ill and angering her.

Their evangelical neighbors grew ever more strident. The new Acilde, still dazed, asked Eric what he was doing when he saw him, with a sporadic pulse, writing symbols on the floors and walls. Startled with a sudden fervor, Eric brought the anemone out of the jar. Acilde was still strapped to the bed and asked for a mirror. Eric didn't have time to explain and knelt by the head of the bed, the anemone's tentacles pointing to Acilde's shaved head. Acilde had a crown of moles, dark spots that made a circle all the way around his head. Eric had noticed it when the girl, now finally in the male form she'd so desired, had knelt before him to suck him off that night at the Mirador.

Acting as a priest now, Eric began to pray in a sharp and nasal voice: "Iba Olokun fe mi lo're. Iba Olokun omo re wa se fun oyío." As he prayed, he joined the tentacles to the moles on Acilde's head. A weak Acilde whimpered and cursed, unable to move. The tentacles stayed put, as though with Velcro, and the marine creature's smell supplanted the neighborhood's garbage stink, transporting Eric back to Matanzas Bay, to the silver lights the sun set moving on the water, and a strong smell of iodine and algae that infused him with the vigor he needed to finish the ritual. "Olokun nuni osi oki elu reye toray. Olokun ni'ka le. Moyugba, Aché." He let go of the creature and brought his face next to Acilde's. "Olokun, here is your child, Eric Vitier, Omioloyu, Omo Yemayá, Okana Di en si Awofaka, paying homage and asking for a blessing." He got even closer to the ear of this newborn man and used his last breath to let him know: "Esther knew what was going to happen. I'm done for. We gave you the body you wanted and now you've given us the body we needed."

COW'S BLOOD

They brought Argenis back to the house looking like a blowfish, his eyes and teeth hidden by the swelling, an allergic reaction to the anemone. Luckily, Linda had an epinephrine pen and gave him an injection. She was aware that the anemone, *Condylactis gigantea*, was in abundance in Playa Bo, but that its poison wasn't enough to do harm unless the person was allergic to it. Hours later, Argenis' face began to turn back to normal, but not before he'd asked Elizabeth to take a photo so he could have a souvenir of himself as this curious monstrosity.

He spent the next week sweating with fever, unable to sleep, and suffering from vertigo that kept him from standing for any amount of time. Malagueta brought over a mattress to sleep in his room and take care of him. His guest entertained Argenis with stories of his childhood in Los Charamicos.

Malagueta was the only one of the artists who was born in Sosúa. As a teenager, he'd been accepted into the baseball academy the Dodgers had on the island, where they educated and trained future major league talents. "But just when I was going to be signed, I screwed up my knee," he explained. He'd stay up all night talking with Argenis about the pitching speeds of his ex-teammates and the stats and whereabouts of those who'd managed to become professional baseball

stars. His long arms and legs were typical of a batter's body, but less so his belly, which he'd cultivated tenderly with Presidente beers and pica pollo. He had a peculiar way with the word "faggot," which he used to refer to everyone, including Argenis: "Drink that soup, faggot; go to sleep, faggot; are you dizzy, faggot?" Argenis thought he was taking it too far, but the guy was taking care of him and he couldn't afford to let things get sour with him.

The mystery as to how this human lump had ended up as a conceptual artist had a lot to do with his love of the Japanese animation they aired on Dominican TV. Malagueta was a fan of *Dragon Ball Z* and as a kid he'd filled seventy notebooks with muscular men with hairy veins and shocking yellow manes floating in a violet or orange sky. When he'd gotten injured, his father – who worked at Giorgio's restaurant – reminded him of his drawing skills, taking him to meet Giorgio and see if he really had talent. Some of Malagueta's photos of Ana Mendieta captured Giorgio's interest. In one, the artist appeared nude and covered in feathers; in another, her silhouette was carved into the ground and set on fire. These strange images were connected with Malagueta's childhood obsession with animated heroes; the body, as it was when on the baseball field, was the protagonist, presenting itself to all who might see it with an elemental and magical fury, like a ball of fire. Not long ago he'd participated in the First Performance Festival in Puerto Plata with a piece called *Home*, in which, standing nude in a batting cage, without a bat or glove, he was hit over and over on his belly and chest by a stream of baseballs from the machine, each coming at him at seventy miles an hour.

During the day, Malagueta worked on his next project – that is, he attended the daily sessions with Iván, worked out, and read about the performance art scene on the internet.

In the afternoons he would work one-on-one with Iván, jotting down even his sighs in his little notebook. These talks took place on a stone bench right in the center of the artists' complex of cabins and Argenis would watch them from his bed like a jealous lover. At noon, Nenuco, the gardener, would bring him pumpkin and yautía soups prepared by Ananí, the woman who worked in the house, and later Ananí herself would bring him chamomile tea so he could get some rest. One morning, Giorgio came in to see how he was doing and to drop off a bunch of materials he'd picked up in the city. Billy didn't want to come in, so he stayed outside, barking, diminishing even further what little love Argenis had for him. When he saw the huge new roll of canvas against the wall, he felt better and told Malagueta he could go back to his own room.

That afternoon, finally free of the vertigo, Argenis sleeps and dreams. He drowns. He flaps around like crazy but can't move; his chest hurts from his violent efforts to breathe in air instead of salt water. On the horizon, an infinite green and gray line of rocks and palms. Several bearded white men with stained clothes approach him in a canoe, pulling him out of the water and taking him to shore. They're carrying knives and antique pistols on their belts and wearing sandals made from braided leather. There's a dark one with very straight black hair who, though he dresses like the others, appears to be Taíno. The only one wearing boots is the one who seems most nervous. He has curly brown hair and wears a long, dark beard. Later, they're in a peasant's hut and they throw Argenis on a leather cot. The Taíno comes in and talks to him in a strange language while the bearded guy in boots brushes the soles of his feet as though he were trying to activate his circulation. There's a smell of meat that wafts in from outside and he wakes up drooling.

After sleeping fourteen whole hours, Argenis felt phenomenal.

At the breakfast table, the conversation touched on the usual themes: art, politics, and environmentalism. John Kelly, the UCLA professor Linda was developing the Playa Bo ecological project with, had joined them that morning and was talking about the increase in the water temperature and the coming crisis that would result from the fatal bleaching of coral in the Caribbean. Argenis was ravenous and putting away his Spanish omelet and garlic toast, catching only bits of information. In his mind, there were fragments of conversations with Malagueta, the dream, and the memory of the moment when he was trapped by the mouth of the rock underwater. Iván got his attention when he said that in the coming weeks they'd be studying Goya and would do an exercise at the end based on the work of the maestro from Aragón. The idea was to complicate the notion of contemporaneity in art and analyze the ways in which Goya, two centuries ago, had articulated his philosophical and formal observations, divorcing himself from the expectations of the work he was commissioned to do and thus inaugurating modern art.

Iván never shut up. He had a special talent for closing down the most disparate and extreme arguments, which had nothing to do with Cuban history, with anecdotes about Cuba, Fernando Ortiz, or Fidel. Argenis was completely out of it. This had happened to him in high school all the time: the teacher would talk and, in his mind, he'd be concocting fantasies, usually sexual and involving classmates, while the teacher, the desk, and his companions all disappeared, lost to the hormonal onslaught of his mental movie. But this was different. He hadn't tried to conjure anything, and he wasn't inventing; he had no control whatsoever over what he was

seeing as clear as a memory. He was once more in the hut from his dreams.

A few men are working on something near the door. The bearded man in boots supervises and gives orders. When he sees Argenis he comes up to him and starts to talk. Argenis can hear his voice. "You're better," he says. Argenis hoped the others heard it too, but they all kept yakking, except Giorgio, who had left the table and was now on the couch out on the terrace reading *Rumbo* magazine. The guy in the boots introduces himself: "I'm Roque, and these are my men." Argenis takes a few steps. He sees what they're doing: pulling the hair from cattle skins, scraping at them with knives while kneeling on the orange dirt.

They're the same guys who pulled him from the sea. "Do you remember your name?" Roque asks. Argenis doesn't dare utter a word; he makes a superhuman effort to focus on what Elizabeth is saying now at the table. She complained that if Goya was modern, then Velázquez was too.

While Ananí brings in the coffee pot, Roque the bearded man tells Argenis he is the only survivor of a shipwreck: "You must have hit your head, that's why you don't remember anything." While Elizabeth puts on a Morcheeba CD out on the terrace, Roque shows him the modest equipment they use to cure the skins from the cattle they hunt inland. While Malagueta digs between his teeth with a wooden toothpick, Argenis gets a nose full of urine, smoke, and flesh in that other place. What the fuck is this? Unlike dreams, with their weird transitions and time portals and stuff like that, the story that's unfolding inside him is coherent and linear.

The others got up from the table to attend the day's session with Iván de la Barra. Argenis remained seated, closing his eyes so he could focus on his internal vision, then extending his right hand to touch Roque and verify the tactile reality

of the bearded man and his world. He touches the warm, damp arm of the man who is now smiling at him and suddenly opened his eyes. He was back at the table, on the terrace, and Giorgio, who had raised his eyes from behind his magazine, had seen him making that strange gesture with his arm while his eyes were closed. Embarrassed, Argenis repeated the movement as if he were trying to get rid of a cramp, afraid Giorgio would think he was crazy. "All those days in bed have fucked up my shoulder," he said, trying to cover his butt, and then ran to catch up with the group.

When they closed the curtains, the living room went dark. Iván turned on the projector and there on the wall was print number sixty-six from *Los caprichos*. "In this series of engravings – besides fusing techniques – Goya presents a subjective satire that cannot be tied to any single reading, destabilizing the sociopolitical paradigms of his time with characters and situations that oscillate between the locally eccentric and the universally mythological." A twisted, androgynous body held a flying broomstick above his head, obscuring the more feminine figure behind him, who also held on to the broomstick and sprouted bat wings to facilitate the magic ride. With Iván still talking in the background, Argenis again closed his eyes. He feels the sun on his skin of that other morning opening up to him.

They're in the hut again, which is a single room with several beds and hammocks. Roque hands him a pair of rough linen pants to wear; that's when Argenis notices he's naked. "If you want to eat, you have to work," Roque says. He hands him a short knife and points to the group curing the skins. "Regardez! Celui qui a survécu à la Côte de Fer," one of the men says as he walks up to them. The man pulls on his pants to make him kneel while showing him what he has to do with the knife on the skin.

When Iván turned on the lights to end the session, Argenis, intent on the involuntary projections in his head, focuses on the skin he's been given to work on. At lunch, Giorgio served some juicy fillets he'd thrown on the terrace grill. The men curing the skins also pause to eat because the Taíno has called them by hitting a rock on a cowbell.

Argenis tried to look calm as he served himself a glass of water from an ice-filled jug, while in his head he is checking out what's going on behind the hut, where strips of meat are being smoked on a green wooden grill. Argenis has seen this before in history books. He brought Giorgio's fillet to his mouth – it was exquisite – but the taste of the hard and salty jerky he was chewing in his other mouth killed his appetite and he ended up leaving both plates untouched. His fellow artists in the Sosúa Project were comparing the PRD and PLD governments: Elizabeth, who was from a family with old money, and not the new stuff politicians took turns stealing, accused both parties of piracy. "Excuse me, but they're all thieves," she said, trying to bait Argenis, whose father was one of them. But it was as if he'd never heard her. The word "pirate" had made him remember Professor Duvergé from fifth grade, when he listed the causes and consequences of Osorio's devastations on the blackboard.

In 1606, Governor Osorio had ordered the depopulation of the island's northern coast to avoid the illegal trade with English, French, and Dutch smugglers, who had been providing the people with what Spain could not. After they were emptied, several towns – among them Puerto Plata, where Sosúa was now – became a refuge for French and English castaways and runaway slaves, the result of abandonment by all military and civilians. They had joined forces to survive, hunting the abandoned cattle, of which there was plenty, to produce leather and smoked meats, which they traded

with the smugglers who still made stops on the coasts. These are buccaneers, thought Argenis, somewhere in the space between the two planes he was now navigating. I can see the past, he said to himself. I'd heard about this but I never imagined it could be like this.

They were supposed to watch a movie, *Goya in Bordeaux*, after lunch, but Iván excused himself so he could talk to Giorgio, and Elizabeth and Malagueta insisted on going into town for a stroll. Los Charamicos was a backwards town, dirty and small, and completely dependent on tourism – in other words, prostitution, in all its varieties. The stroll was short and boring: a bunch of little wooden stalls with Haitian paintings, towels, and souvenirs with the words "Sosúa No Problem." Argenis dropped back and walked alone, resuming his work curing the skins while very aware of the rugged faces of the people working around him on the other side of his mind. The Taíno was a man of blunt movements who'd just started to go gray; the man who'd said "Côte de Fer" was blond with a narrow back, a prominent chin, and a fuzzy peach mustache. There was also a one-armed man with black hair and a beard, a black man they called Engombe, and Roque. They were all bags of bone and sinew, encased in skin that had been marbled by permanent sunburn.

Elizabeth was recording their outing through the neighborhood ruins with one of her cameras to "document" their visit, while Malagueta greeted a few people who recognized him. For a moment Argenis set aside the curing of skins in his parallel world and felt a sudden embarrassment. What were they doing strolling like kings through a poor neighborhood? Fucking cultural tourists. "Allez, allez," says the blond buccaneer, urging him to cure another skin, but Argenis was too busy feeling out of place in 2001 Sosúa. What would happen if I didn't do what they asked? As though he'd heard

his question, Engombe punches him in the ear, which frees him of embarrassments and distractions. He picks up the knife and starts anew, fearful the black man will hit him again. I'm screwed, he thinks. Where do I turn off this shit? On their way back to Playa Bo, Argenis pretended he'd fallen asleep in Elizabeth's car so he could finish peeling his skin. Afterward, they give him a little jug of moonshine that he drinks while leaning on a guayacán tree, watching the black man stack the smoked meats, now cold, in a barrel. The sun is going down for the buccaneers, with the same tones in the sky as in Playa Bo, and for Argenis two suns dropped below the horizon. Experiencing these two realities at once was like putting together a jigsaw puzzle on the table while watching the news on TV. The news was his present, predictable and harmless; the world of the buccaneers was the jigsaw puzzle he had to focus on, lifting his head now and again without dropping any pieces. The two suns didn't compete for his attention, instead appearing one on top of the other, like stacked negatives. When they vanished, and with them his strange internal movie, Argenis felt relief and fear in equal parts. But the worry and curiosity about what had happened lasted as long as the excitement over an interesting dream. He dragged a chair over to the cliff. Alone, he took in and savored the blackening view. Iván and Giorgio were drinking wine out on the lightless terrace, listening to a recording of John Cage talking about a tie. Someone lit a candle and the light attracted Argenis, who saw from afar the illuminated face of his prosperous patron. He followed the black line of Giorgio's mouth and jaw, calculating the colors he'd need to mix to achieve the brick tones that the flame gave his skin. It had been a very long time since he'd looked at anyone the way he was looking at Giorgio now, translating every detail his eyes perceived into the technical steps he'd need to make

a facsimile. In his mind, Argenis was already painting, and then he rushed toward them. "Don't move," he ordered. He darted back to his cabin, imagining how he would apply the perfect color already mixed, and selected the tubes he'd need. He returned to the cliff with a chair, the small easel he'd had since high school, and the battery-powered lamp he'd clamped on the side. He turned his back to the sea to arrange his instruments, looking at the terrace. A jungle of palms, sea grapes, and almond trees framed the house in a cloud of deep gray. An intense black broke only in the very center, where Giorgio Menicucci, his precise features and body lost in the gloom, had become an igneous mask floating in the air. In front of it, Argenis decided to paint another face: his own, the one he'd worn after the accident with the anemone, the one Elizabeth had photographed. The face lit by the candle was haughty and beautiful; it seemed to be giving an order with which the deformed monster, given the inclination of its head, would comply.

Unfortunately for Argenis, the buccaneers returned the next day. As soon as he opened his eyes, the strange handle that seemed to let the ghosts into his head began to turn and, just like the day before, everything was connected and real. He stayed in his cabin, trying to get rid of the visions by taking deep breaths, doing push-ups, taking cold showers. Nothing worked against the Taíno, who passes around a bucket of milk, nor the black man, who leads him to a rough basin where the little French guy greets him once more: ". . . qui a survécu à la Côte de Fer." He's using a paddle to stir the peeled skins in a dark liquid. Argenis grabs another paddle and copies the French guy's movements. The black man watches him with a tight fist but Argenis is doing a pretty good job. Concentrating on that one repetitive activity and now seriously concerned, he decided to step out of his room.

When he got to Iván's workshop (he was late), there was a photogram on the screen from Matthew Barney's *Cremaster 2*, in which Norman Mailer played Houdini.

Professor Herman had dedicated an entire class to Barney's work. Iván de la Barra noted the connection between his installations, videos, and sculpture, and Goya's work, their shared sensibility for the sublimely terrible and the elaboration of mythologies rooted in popular culture. Iván had seen *Cremaster 2* in Madrid at the Reina Sofía the year before and Elizabeth had seen it in Chicago in 1999. Malagueta had never left the island and Argenis had only been as far as Cuba, to a camp for the children of revolutionaries, so they had to make do with Iván's narration. Iván explained that the cremaster is the muscle that lifts and lowers the testicles and responds to changes in temperature; the narrative thread that runs through all five films in the cycle is the process of sexual differentiation in the embryo. In *Cremaster 2*, the organism resists differentiation, resulting in a drama that, according to Iván, plays out like a surreal western while creating a poetic biography of the American killer Gary Gilmore. "In a spectacular exercise of free association, Gilmore was executed in 1977; he was the first person to be condemned to death after capital punishment was reinstated in the United States. Gilmore's father was supposedly the son of a famous magician who passed through Sacramento, possibly Houdini. Gilmore's mother was a Mormon, and the honeycomb is a Mormon symbol." Iván was writing all this on the blackboard. "What Barney is doing is sifting through this information with an aesthetic proposition that blurs the usual connections that symbol and ritual make," said the Cuban as he clicked through to show other photograms.

The skins are now free of hair and flesh and nearing their final color and texture at the bottom of a basin filled with

alum and salt. The little French guy plucks an unshelled peanut from his pocket and eats it. His hands, blackened by work and the lack of hygiene, are much more real to Argenis than Iván's efforts to make Barney's films a work of genius. After the workshop, Argenis accompanied Malagueta to look for a book on *Cremaster 2* in Giorgio and Linda's library, a bookcase three meters tall in the living room. While Malagueta climbed a chair to reach the book, Argenis glanced over the collection and was surprised to find a shelf filled with volumes on buccaneers, Osorio's devastations, and pirates and smuggling in the Caribbean. This kind of coincidence ought to have a name. Whenever he heard a word for the first time, a stream of references, information, and associations would rise up out of nowhere, as though the universe were conjuring up the tools necessary for learning, or as though it were giving its approval to a specific path of knowledge. Linda was on the terrace and Malagueta went over to her to let her know he was taking the book to his cabin and that Argenis, too, was borrowing some books. After the incident with the anemone, Argenis had reacted like a cat stung by frog venom and avoided Linda as much as possible. "Giorgio said you painted something incredible last night," she said as she caressed Billy with her big toe. "Can I see it?" At any other time, Argenis would have taken Linda to his studio, thinking about his dick coming in and out of her beautiful ass the whole way there. But something had happened in the water and now he felt a strange repulsion connecting the libidinous desires that drove him into the nest of anemones with the resulting disagreeable experience.

Once in his studio, she was quite pleased with the painting. "It's excellent," she said, then, winking at him, she added: "If there's a disaster that destroys technology, electricity,

and digital files, your work will survive. What would happen to the work of all of those video artists and performance artists?"

Linda Menicucci had an apocalyptic way of thinking about things and treated everything, even works of art, like species to be measured for their capacity to survive on earth. She had agreed to sponsor these artists because her husband had assured her they would recover their investment and the profits would help push forward her environmental protection project for Playa Bo. Giorgio and Linda were thinking about buying several more kilometers of beach and continuing the research to identify all the species that lived in the coral reef. Although government laws protected areas of the reef, the lack of resources made it practically impossible to enforce them, leaving hundreds of species at the mercy of indiscriminate fishing, construction, and contamination. Argenis now understood Linda was only interested in him for one reason, the same reason he was interested in her and Giorgio: money. She needed it to save her little fish and Argenis to realize his fantasy of future happiness: a life snorting coke, painting, and paying sluts so they would suck him off without anyone giving him a hard time.

In this way, Argenis and this high-class woman were equals. Argenis would have enjoyed this small victory more if it wasn't for the fact that, in his other life, he was being forced to pull the skins from the basin to air them out: it required almost all his attention. During the three hours the process involves, his arms begin to tremble; the black guy, Engombe, as always, waits for him. He walked Linda to the door and saw her in this new light. He could make out the lines the sun and her excessive concern for her cause – a lost cause, as far as Argenis was concerned – had drawn on her face. He closed the door, glanced at the clock to confirm

it was lunchtime, and threw himself in bed. He quickly fell asleep, fried.

Immune to sleep, the buccaneers continue. After hanging and massaging the skins, Roque, who had disappeared for most of the day, comes out of the northern thicket with the one-armed man, announcing that there's an English galleon on the coast and they will meet with the crew the next day. He pulls two bottles of wine from the bag on his shoulder as proof and a shirt, which he tosses to Argenis. "Regardez, survivant à la Côte de Fer . . ." says the little French guy, who doesn't have a name for him, and gestures for him to put on the shirt. They drink, passing the bottles from one to another in the warmth of the fire prepared by the Taíno, who takes great pains to offer the best pieces of cassava and pork to Argenis, whose eyes are shutting in that world just as he is due to wake in this one.

It looked like this nuisance was going to be around for the long haul and there was no way for Argenis to disconnect himself. Unlike the previous night, this time the visions had left him full of questions. Was this a past incarnation? Was it schizophrenia? Witchcraft? If his patrons ever found out about this they would kick him out of the project, and then he knew he'd really go crazy, out of his mind, full-on wacko at his mom's house.

Oh shut up, he told himself, and stepped into the fresh night air of Playa Bo with Esquemelin's *Buccaneers of America* under his arm, following the sound of music coming from the terrace. As he crossed the row of dwarf palms dividing the cabins from the house, he got a whiff of the marijuana Iván and Giorgio were smoking as they whispered together. He had promised himself he'd stay away from coke for the duration of the project, but he wasn't going to say no to a little pot. When he saw Argenis coming, Giorgio stood up, a

little nervously. "Monsieur, try this," he said, passing him a joint and catching sight of the book Argenis had set on the table. "You like that? This place was full of buccaneers," he said, with a gesture to suggest as far as the eye could see. "Must be full of ghosts." Iván had a Word document open on his laptop that read: "Notes for Olokun," in a font that looked like Helvetica Bold. When he closed the document, the screen showed the first engraving from *The Disasters of War* as his wallpaper. "Do you like this engraving?" he asked without looking up from the screen. Argenis explained that he'd taken engraving classes and had worked on his technique in school, but he'd never made a professional series of prints. By then Giorgio had filled Argenis' glass and was raising his own for a toast: "That the spirits of the buccaneers will bring us luck!" Argenis was on his second toke of the hydroponic grass, which was much more potent than he was used to, and it hit him hard. Giorgio was talking about the adventures of a friend of his who'd spent the last twenty years combing the beaches of Puerto Plata with a metal detector, looking for treasure left by the pirate Cofresí. His friend had dumped his wife and abandoned his kids, his job, convinced that one day he would find the loot buried somewhere by the great plunderer. Rapt, Iván coughed from too much laughter. "Dude, what an asshole!" he said. Argenis opened the book to a random page so he could focus on something and avoid their looks, because he felt on the verge of a panic attack. In his narrative about the lives of the pirates and buccaneers of America, Esquemelin had included the code that protected injured pirates: "For the loss of an eye, one hundred escudos or one slave. For the loss of the right hand, two hundred escudos or two slaves. For the loss of two feet or two legs, six hundred escudos or six slaves." The reading competed with the associations Argenis was making in

his mind: They are referring to me, I'm never going to get ahead, the dead buccaneers have come to find me, Goya's engravings are a sign: they are going to mutilate me. And on it went. Giorgio noticed Argenis was not doing well. "Maestro, relax." He stood behind him and started to rub his neck. These faggots are going to rape me, thought Argenis, that's why Iván said 'asshole'; goddamn pot. Giorgio's massage began to take effect and a heaviness came over every part of his body, sound vibrations overwhelmed his interior dialogue and produced a silence punctuated by a low and heavy hum. He experienced a few fleeting holograms. In one he was a little boy running towards his father, there to pick up Argenis and his brother for an obligatory biweekly visit. When his father lifted him up, Argenis grabbed his head with both hands and kissed him on the mouth. His father threw him violently on the ground, looking around them in all directions. "Are you a faggot, huh?" He felt again the equal parts of pain and fear he'd felt that afternoon, as the tiny particles of light that made up the memory vanished, victims to a miraculous dispersal. He opened his eyes and the massage was over. Giorgio was squatting in front of the stereo to change the CD and Iván was tying up the trash bag next to the grill to take it out. "Man, if we leave this here, it's going to attract flies."

Argenis came to understand that the buccaneers would let him be at night but would claim the day, even his daydreams, so he decided to wait until the sun came up to go to bed. He was mentally exhausted and he didn't give a damn about Iván's theories concerning Goya. As soon as he fell asleep, he found himself among Roque's men, walking through a scrubland of sea grapes and brambles.

The one-armed man cuts a path with the scimitar in his good hand. They're hauling one hundred skins in rolls of ten,

two barrels of jerky, one bag of salt, and some sweet potatoes. They cross the last of the vegetation and find themselves on an ash-colored reef, heading west. They reach a cliff and climb down with the goods. They're in Playa Bo. The Menicuccis' beach is almost unrecognizable, the sea full of shoals, fish swimming in circles in the hundreds, some a meter long that could be pulled from the water by hand. A galleon with its sails furled is anchored a short distance from the coast and two small rowboats approach to pick them up.

Once on deck, the captain – an Englishman with clean nails and yellow teeth who has just sacked a Spanish rescue ship en route to New Spain – goes over the list of things Roque requested in exchange for the skins. Twenty bottles of wine, a sack of wheat flour, two pairs of boots, two felt hats, a trunk, gunpowder, buckles, two long arquebuses, and a sort of table the three men struggle to lift out of the porthole. The captain removes the canvas from it to reveal a printing press.

With the press come three rolls of paper, three wooden plates, and everything needed to make an engraving, except ink.

They complete the deal. Roque promises to bring the captain one hundred more skins once he returns from Bayamo, Cuba, where the people – who've been abandoned by the Spanish policy that only Havana and Santiago can receive commercial ships – will welcome him as a hero. It takes them half the day to transport the heavy machine to the hut. Roque meets the complaints by explaining that the Spanish residents on the island, as needy as the people of Bayamo, will want to buy it for much more than they paid for it. The Taíno, who had stayed behind to keep guard over their settlement, welcomes them back with joy and tells them there are two hundred heads of cattle in a nearby clearing. His Spanish is clumsy and only Roque can understand him. With the others,

he acts like the fallen cacique he probably is. Roque orders the construction of another hut to house the press. The one-armed man and the little French guy pick up their axes and head south looking for wood. Roque, Engombe, and Argenis start for the place where the Taíno has seen the cattle, armed with one of the new arquebuses, a bottle of wine, and several knives. Without a word, Engombe, who carries the arquebus, separates from the group and stealthily makes his way east. A few steps ahead of them, Roque and Argenis can see the animals, grazing at the foot of a hill, and Engombe, who has reached the far right side of the slope and is loading his gun to begin the slaughter.

Argenis woke up at the first shot. With a feeling of dismay and excitement, he sat up, watching how the cattle fell to the bullets Engombe was pumping, at close range, into their heads. Those that were still alive, stupid and heavy, ran in circles. Roque explained that they would flay a few of them now, that tomorrow the cattle would return to graze in the same place and they'd slaughter a few more then. Engombe and Roque worked on the dead cattle quickly and with precision, slashing from the throat to the anus and then from one leg to another. When all the cattle had been opened up, they began to peel the skins, with the help of Argenis, who took notes with a piece of charcoal and a piece of fabric he'd unrolled on the floor of his workshop. With his vision clouded with the hot smell of blood, which was beginning to clot in the faraway pasture, he reached for the Cadmium Red, squeezing the tube of Winsor & Newton straight onto the brush like toothpaste.

THE GARDENER

With the water so clear, it was easy to pull out octopuses, starfish, and sea snails from under the rocks. Willito had come alone because none of his homies would dare go to Nenuco's beach. The last time the group had gone fishing there, Pachico had wound up with a shot in the ass, the cops telling them they were on Nenuco's property and he had the right to fire on them.

Nenuco was a real bastard, with more fish in his waters than he and his family could possibly eat or sell, and Willito had two little brothers and a sick grandfather. He supported them by selling whatever he could find on the coral reefs to the gift shops and restaurants in Sosúa.

The pool formed by the reefs on Playa Bo was full of animal life because, unlike the others, it had a madman with a shotgun who wouldn't let anyone near. It's better this way, thought Willito. Alone, with a wetsuit, fins, and a harpoon, he'd make very little noise.

He'd left the house at five in the morning, when it was still dark. He skirted the coast in his grandfather's skiff, leaving it anchored behind a crag so he could leap and swim over to that trove of natural treasures at the first ray of light. Willito had been there three times before; he knew how to get to the reef underwater, through a hole in

a rock several meters long and two feet wide. Pachico had shown him how to swim through it without getting stung by the anemones.

Willito was wearing a belt with weights so he wouldn't float. He moved quickly, propelled by the fins, holding the harpoon with both hands until he reached the mouth of the rock and saw a body, a dead body, in the hole. His fear was greater than the weights and he shot up to the surface, splashing and screaming as though he didn't know how to swim. His vision blurred by water, Willito saw Nenuco in his underwear, standing on the reef and pointing at him with his shotgun. "There's a body in the hole, Nenuco, don't kill me," he yelled.

"Get out of here," said Nenuco, with his broad forehead and slanted eyes. "Go before I blow your brains out, you son of a fucking whore." Willito reached his skiff in just three strokes, with a fear that had nothing to do with Nenuco's shotgun. He told Pachico, who still had a limp, what he'd seen and they went back to the local officials, trying to sell the idea that Nenuco had killed somebody and hidden the body in the hole. Corporal Fonso didn't give them the time of day until, after a week of nonstop pestering, he decided to go take a look.

Fonso had never liked Nenuco. To his mind, Nenuco might have been the owner of the land at Playa Bo but water was nobody's property. In spite of that, his supervisors had made it crystal clear that Nenuco had people in government and Fonso couldn't mess with him. Nenuco's property had three parcels of land on the coast. They were partly fertile black earth where his family grew plantains, cassava, squash, and avocados, and partly red dirt and reef with an abundance of almond trees, sea grapes, and coconut trees. In fact, the real owner of the land was Ananí, Nenuco's cousin, whom he had

married. She was very small, black, with cinnamon skin and very straight black hair she'd inherited from her parents.

The coconut trunks that grew along the path to Playa Bo had been painted red, with white letters spelling out "Balaguer 90-94," vestiges of the most recent electoral campaign. Nenuco's fence posts were painted the governing party's colors, too, and the door of the house had a photo of the "Doctor" giving a speech. Fonso parked his Honda 70 at the edge of the house and, taking off his hat, greeted a woman who was cleaning rice in a bowl as she swayed in a rocking chair by the door. "What do you want?" said Ananí. She picked out a bad grain and threw it toward his feet. "I came to talk with Nenuco," said Fonso, peeking in at the tiny kitchen, which smelled of fresh fish and lemon. Nenuco was cleaning a grouper skillfully and tossed its roe at the floor for a ginger cat. At the back of the living room, a young woman was watching *El Gordo de la Semana* on TV. A contestant was throwing the Knorr Lucky Dice, trying to win a refrigerator, an electric knife, or a toaster. "Did someone complain about me, Fonso?"

"Those boys make up a lot of stuff," he said, feeling like an idiot.

"So what did they make up now?" Nenuco asked, leaving his task to pick up a pewter cup and offer the officer some coffee.

"Crazy stuff," said Fonso, who drank the coffee without bringing the subject up again, talking instead about the week's local news: the old people who'd died, the mothers who'd given birth, and a machete fight that had broken out when someone put up a fence a meter farther than what had been agreed. For his part, Nenuco told the corporal about the new mansions the Russians and Australians were building all over Puerto Plata, where he'd been working for years as a

gardener to help with the family's cash flow. Nenuco's son, who had slanted eyes like his father and long hair like his mother, brought over a bunch of green plantains and a bag of cassava for the corporal, as he had been trained to do when they had company. Fonso thanked him and asked to use the latrine. Next to the wooden structure near the back of the house, he saw a cement basin painted blue and filled with a white liquid. Piled by the basin were the young coconuts from which they'd stripped the meat. What do they need so much milk for? Fonso asked himself as he tied the bunch of plantains to the back of the Honda 70.

As soon as the roar of Fonso's motor had faded, Nenuco abandoned his chores and ran to the back bedroom, where a man lay covered with a white sheet on a bed raised by four cement blocks. A cemí made of yellow cotton and attached to a trembling string hung over the body. There was a cross and a circle drawn in chalk on the untreated wood that made up the back wall. A line snaked diagonally from the center of the cross. If the corporal had come in here, thought Nenuco, he would have run away in horror, people are that stupid. He lifted up the man, who was half asleep, and draped him across his shoulders to help him walk. Out in the yard, Ananí knelt before their naked guest, who was approaching while leaning on her husband. She spoke to him with the words she'd been taught, words she knew she had to use to receive the one who came from the water: "Bayacú Bosiba Guamikeni." They eased his body into the cement basin with utmost care. Then they submerged him up to his neck and poured coconut milk on the moles that circled the top of his head.

Ananí had been born in water, but not like the Great Lord they now bathed; he had not been born of woman. Mama Guama, the old blind woman who still lived with them, had given birth to Ananí in a pool at Playa Bo all by herself.

73

Ananí's father, Jacinto Guabá, had disappeared on orders from Trujillo, who wanted to take his land and add them to those he was giving the Jews to whom he'd offered refuge during the great war. In the end, something made Trujillo reconsider and he left them with a quarter of what they had once had, including Playa Bo.

Since then, Ananí had wanted nothing to do with politics. Nenuco had to convince her to not spurn the gifts the current president sent from the city. At Christmas, a van with the party logo would show up, filled with sacks of rice, wine, apples, chocolate, bikes, balls and dolls for the kids, and some electric appliances. The gifts would be accompanied by a card addressed to Princess Ananí and signed by his Excellency, asking for her blessing. Her response was always the same: she'd tear the card and throw the pieces in the latrine before ordering Nenuco to distribute everything among the neighbors, except for the toys, which she kept for her own kids, Guaroa and Yararí.

She didn't accept the gifts because she believed Balaguer was complicit in her father's death, and she tore up the cards because she didn't want anything to do with letters; Ananí always said they were pure lies, trash. When she was little and it became compulsory to go to school, Ananí learned her letters and numbers. She loved to look at the images of her ancestors in the illustrated history books, hunting, sowing, fishing, and dancing the areíto, though she knew what was written in those books wasn't true. The books said there were fewer than six hundred Taínos by 1531 and that, a little later, they had completely disappeared. Her family, descended from caciques and behíques, had survived, like many others in the Republic they'd stayed in contact with to marry their young people and enact their rituals. The books said nothing of the men from the water, who came every so often to help them,

nor of the Spanish, who'd stolen power from the Arawaks to conquer the other tribes on the continent. Ananí had been taught never to speak of these things with anyone, and she had always complied with that order. She left school in fourth grade. Nenuco made it to eighth grade; his parents had said that to deal with those who were sleeping, you had to know what they were thinking.

Nenuco was born in Barahona, on the southern part of the island, where his father, Ananí's uncle, had gone on to marry a descendant of Enriquillo. In 1973, when he was seventeen, his parents had sent Nenuco on a bus with a sack of clothes, a golden vest, a machete, some shears to cut grass with, and the family cemí, to marry his cousin.

The first thing he did when he got to Playa Bo was plant flowers in front of the house, red, yellow, and white blooms that grew with the health and beauty of everything Nenuco planted in the earth. He didn't speak directly, only through Mama Guama, and only about the garden, which he slowly brought to life all around the house.

Even amidst the dryness of the beach, the garden blossomed in the shade of the almond trees, roses, bromeliads, dwarf palms, and ferns, which Nenuco brought from the gardens he tended so beautifully in the houses and hotels where he found work. When she was ready to be in love, Ananí gave him a clay potiza in the shape of a heart, from whose breasts emerged a penis as a symbol of their union: they would cease being male and female to become one single beating organism.

Beyond their love and their children, what united them was taking care of the Great Lord, Playa Bo, where the most precious and sacred creature on the island dwelled, the portal to the land of the beginning, through which the men of the water would come, the big heads, whenever they were needed.

That was why every summer Nenuco would pay special attention to the pool, monitoring the tunnel with the anemones where the phenomenon took place.

Their supervision had become routine until one day when, during the night, a blister about a foot long broke out on the main anemone. Mama Guama, blind now, came down every evening with Nenuco to play a gourd and give thanks to Yocahú, the creator, for letting her live so she could experience the miracle. Nenuco would sleep on the beach with a shotgun on his shoulder to protect the nest from the boys who hoped to sneak in to fish at first light; their hooks and harpoons could hurt the envoy, as fragile as an embryo in the water.

Willito had had the misfortune of running into that half-finished body, but Nenuco hadn't killed him because he knew his grandfather and prayed the boy wouldn't go talk all over town.

Yararí was fourteen years old and sick of all the ceremony and weird stuff. She didn't want to belong to her parents' world of mystery and whispers and had convinced Ananí to keep the Sony Trinitron TV Balaguer had sent her the previous Christmas. She didn't convince her exactly: she'd threatened to kill herself if Ananí said no. In the afternoons, she'd ride by the houses of the rich on her bike and pretend she lived in one of them. Unlike her brother, she didn't know a single word of Taíno and she loved school, especially her English teacher, who was a gringo priest with blue eyes. When Nenuco came home from the beach one afternoon with a man in his arms and asked everyone to help him, she stayed on the couch, feet up, watching the Coco Band play live on *Súper Tarde* on Channel 9. "Girl, turn that down," Mama Guama begged her. Yararí, full of malice, turned the volume up a little: "I already did," she said. The worst part was she and Guaroa

now had to sleep on the hammocks in the living room to give their room to the damned sick man. She was sure the guy was just a drunk tourist her father had rescued from the waves, even if her parents had spent a lifetime telling her otherwise. Yararí would choose what she wanted to believe, and every time she bruised her knuckles washing her father and brother's pants, she'd curse her mother for having given away the Korean washing machine she'd received as a gift alongside the TV. She was hanging clothes on the fence when Willito, whose curiosity had not been satisfied by Fonso's visit, passed in front of her on a mule. He'd seen her before at school in town, slender and vibrant, with still-growing breasts and that black mane kissing her ass. She didn't even glance at him; she dismissed him because he was riding an animal. Willito realized this. The next day he rode past on a Sanyang motorbike he'd borrowed, except this time Yararí wasn't outside and didn't see him, though Nenuco did, and wondered if the little thief was still trying to find out more about what he'd seen at the reef.

We have to speed this up, the gardener said to himself. That night, while everyone slept, he took a hand mirror over to the guest's room; the man had dropped the scales from his eyes and was now sitting up on the edge of the bed. "We've been waiting for you," Nenuco said in a very gentle voice. "You came from far away, bright star of the waters, and now I'm going to help you remember." The man said nothing. He seemed scared, confused, and moved his eyes around all over the place, as though he were seeing things that weren't in the room with them. Nenuco put the mirror in his hand and guided it in front of his face, with its wide jaw and dark brow. "Where am I?" the man asked in a sweet and raspy voice. "You're in Playa Bo, in Sosúa, in the Dominican Republic." He tried to get up but he still didn't have the strength. Nenuco

made him get back in bed, turning on the pedestal fan and switching the electric light as he left.

The man's gaze went past his penis, which rested on his testicles, to the window in front of the bed, where the smell of the Atlantic came in to penetrate the darkened room. The waves roared against the cliff and the recurring sound brought him the image of a woman bleeding from her belly and looking at him with both resignation and urgency. "Esther Escudero," he said, without knowing what that meant, although he discovered a certain familiarity in his own voice. The marine smells brought other memories: an animal with tentacles at the bottom of a jar, a steaming coffee pot, a penis entering his mouth. "Esther Escudero," he said again, and the resonance of his voice in his body made him aware of its limits and those of the objects around him. He repeated the name several times. It was as though the letters of that name were fishing hooks searching the depths of his mind as he captured fragments of images that, just as they were taking shape, would once more dissolve. "Fan," he said, watching the blades on the machine turn and turn as he got up, naked, and started toward the light in the living room. Yararí was sitting on the couch watching TV. Al Pacino had just ordered pizza for his hostages in *Dog Day Afternoon*. The man sat down next to her, looked curiously at the small screen, the furniture, the pots and pans hanging from nails on the kitchen walls, and the 1991 Nestlé calendar. Without taking her eyes off the movie, Yararí closed her fingers around his olive-colored penis and pumped it rhythmically with her right hand; when it got hard she took off her panties and sat on top of him, never taking her eyes off the TV, using her hand to guide him inside her and then moving up and down as he directed her with his hands on her waist. In minutes he'd filled her with cum. A cold sensation in his head brought

the past rushing back. Just before he'd come, he'd seen Eric Vitier's face telling him: "You're the chosen one," as though he were completely drunk, followed by the foamy, coherent recollection of his days back in the Santo Domingo of 2027. In the same way he'd muttered the name of the priestess before, he now pronounced his own: "Acilde Figueroa," and his mind, reacting to it like a password, made all its contents accessible as the daughter of his hosts put her panties back on and changed the channel.

UPDATE

Do I have two bodies or is my mind capable of broadcasting two different channels simultaneously? Acilde asked himself, his eyes fixed on the small fake-pearl necklace worn by the nurse who was changing his IV. The day's news was being projected in front of his hospital bed: "During a raid in Villa Mella, after a tip from the leaders of the Pentecostal terrorists, the Servants of the Apocalypse, the Special Police accidentally rounded up one of the suspects in the murder of Esther Escudero, an Africanist religious leader and personal friend of the president, murdered last week during a robbery of her home. The suspect, Acilde Figueroa, who according to her digital footprint was a woman, is now a man, and was found strapped to a bed, unconscious and dehydrated, next to the corpse of Dr. Eric Vitier, who appeared to have suffered respiratory failure hours before. Authorities also found a sea anemone, valued at sixty-five thousand dollars. The specimen has been transferred to a private laboratory, where it is currently receiving specialized care." Photos of a happy Acilde, Eric, Esther, and Morla that had nothing to do with the news appeared on the screen during the voiceover: Acilde at a birthday party, Eric at his medical school graduation in Cuba, and a selfie of Morla in a yellow Indiana Pacers T-shirt.

A helicopter landed noisily on the roof of the hospital. Outside Acilde's room, next to the half-open door, the police officer keeping guard swatted away mosquitos with his hand as he watched a baseball game on an old tablet. Acilde walked to the bathroom unassisted. He lifted the hospital robe to look at himself in the mirror, pleased with the results of the drug: the new broadness to his back and thickness to his forearms, the absence of fat from his hips, the sad little sac holding his balls, and a chest so flat it was incapable of nourishing another human being. He thought the late twentieth-century life in Sosúa playing out in his head might be a side effect of the Rainbow Brite. Back in Sosúa, in the little house where the natives revered him, in front of the mirror that hung from a nail over the faucet in the yard, he assured himself, like a midwife with a newborn, that this new body didn't need anything else. It's identical, he thought, entranced, as he pinched the nipples and buttocks and opened and closed the mouth of this 1991 version of himself, and said, "I'm hungry," then ate with his fingers from the cold fish a hopeful Nenuco offered him on a Duralex dish.

Satisfied, he made his way back to the hospital bed. The officer at the door opened it with the formality and efficiency of someone being watched by his superiors. A huge red-haired mulato, in a very red Adidas tracksuit and with a Holy Infant of Atocha medal hanging from his neck on a gold chain, came in with two suited bodyguards. He snapped his fingers to make them leave, then dropped onto the couch.

He bit a nail and spit it out. "So then, you're the little queer who's going to save the country?" he asked. Acilde did not respond. He made his way to the bed with effort, embarrassed by the little robe in which the President of

the Republic had surprised him. "Esther Escudero was my sister, you little faggot," he said, closing his fist. He was making Acilde nervous, with his voice like Balaguer's and face like Malcolm X. "I'm not ordering them to break your ass because I promised her, I swore to her, that no matter what happened we would give you whatever you needed to realize your mission."

It seemed the entire world, past and present, was expecting something very important from him and, in front of Said Bona, Acilde felt an urgent need to pretend he knew what they were talking about. This man had captured the country's will for fifteen years and his charisma had the same effect on Acilde as on the masses he had seduced via YouTube videos in which he criticized the government and used Dominican street Spanish. Once in power, Said had declared himself a socialist, signing a bunch of treaties with the Latin American Bolivarian Alliance, which was pursuing its dream of a Great Colombia in each of its totalitarian member states. He imprisoned all the corrupt ex-government bureaucrats with real charges, and used false charges against the leaders of the opposition. He expropriated companies and properties, celebrating his first anniversary in power by changing the party's colors from purple and yellow to red and black, in honor of Legbá, Elegguá, the African deity who ruled his destiny, Lord of the Four Paths and messenger of the gods, and declaring Dominican voodoo and all its mysteries as the official religion.

But now Said Bona was in a tight spot. After he agreed to warehouse Venezuelan biological weapons in Ocoa, the 2024 seaquake had done away with the base where they'd been kept and dispersed their contents into the Caribbean sea. Entire species had vanished in a matter of weeks. The environmental crisis had spread to the Atlantic.

As he lost support, Said struggled to accuse the United States and the European Union of having fabricated the tsunami with the goal of destabilizing the region.

Acilde intuited that the task they wanted him to take on had something to do with that disaster, which had made Esther Escudero cry during her morning prayers. It was because of that disaster that oceanographers and doctors were streaming into the country and the Caribbean was a dark and putrid stew. Said used his index finger to touch the tip of his huge Dolce & Gabbana glasses and a hologram of Esther Escudero materialized next to the bed. Omicunlé was wearing a white dress with a long and broad skirt, a dark blue turban, and the infinite number of necklaces and bracelets appropriate to her priestly vocation. She looked like what Acilde imagined her ghost would look like. "If you're seeing this, it means everything's gone well," said the ghost, smiling and calm. "Eric initiated you and now you know you are Omo Olokun: the one who knows what lies at the bottom of the sea. Said depends on me, so use the powers you have begun to discover for the good of humanity. Save the sea, Maferefún Olokun, Maferefún Yemayá." The message over and the ghost gone, Said took off his glasses and discovered his eyes were wet, the very same eyes that had so delighted the women of the nation when, impassioned during the electoral campaign, he'd declared that the children of single mothers were children of the mother country and, as such, his children. "What do you need?" Said asked Acilde, now with respect.

Because of the discreet and unspecific way in which Esther had referred to his powers, he understood he had no need to reveal the window to the past that had opened in his mind, nor the clone there whom he maneuvered by remote control. So far, this was his only power, and he

wanted to test the reality of the past he'd reached with the anemone he'd once thought of selling for mere cents. "I need a quiet and private place, because these are the Days of Remembering, in which I will recover the memory of my past lives and of my mission," said Acilde, using the ceremonious language of those who had pulled him from the waters in 1991 and awakening the president's curiosity for the first time.

They came to an agreement: Acilde would go to jail for a few months to calm down the followers of Esther who were asking for his head. Said would guarantee his stint was pleasant and later, after finding incontrovertible proof of his innocence, would set him free.

Acilde's cell had a toilet, a sink, an oven, a little fridge, a bed, and a table with an old forty-four-inch monitor connected to a keyboard. On the gray, carpeted floor there was a handprint with orange specks, as though someone had dumped a sardine and rice dish there for a couple of days. He was not allowed a data plan in jail because hackers might be able to detect it and accuse the government of favoring certain prisoners. While there, Acilde rested for most of the day now that the man he'd started to become in Sosúa had started to move at his command. He learned many things about that time and its people and he got a good idea of what was expected of him. A month after he had arrived, Nenuco had already shared with him all he knew: the portal with the anemones, the name of all the animals in the pool in both Spanish and Taíno, recipes for cooking them, the purpose and origin of all of the herbs they grew in the yard, and the nature of the other world that Acilde was from. Acilde let Nenuco fantasize because, if he realized the other world was a prison cell in 2027, he would have put a bullet in his brain.

Yararí had run off with Willito and they'd heard she was pregnant. As soon as he kidnapped her, Willito had her cooking what he fished with a little net at the beach. Nenuco had gone to get her but the girl told him she was never going back to that "damned shack ever again."

During the day, Acilde would lie in bed with his eyes closed so his other self could run around Sosúa on the back of Nenuco's motorcycle, asking questions and taking notes of the street and business names, the names of people, with the excuse that he was writing a book. In the darkness of his cell, he would compare these notes on the old computer he had been allowed to have. When he entered the names from his notes in the search engine, he'd get lots of historical information: the success of certain businesses, the misfortune of others, the future criminality of an innocent-seeming young man or the promotion to mayor of an illiterate woman. How lost and obtuse the people of that small town looked now, how sad their small plans and projections, how comedic the desperation of someone who does not yet know a marvelous destiny awaits around the corner.

He had still not been able to confirm his own existence in the historical Sosúa, nor that his double had been there among its people and that, like everybody else, he'd left a mark. To confirm his presence he needed to be someone, he needed a name, he needed papers, and so that very night Nenuco took him to see Stephan, a German who owned a bar and falsified documents for Europeans with dubious pasts who'd retired in Sosúa with the kind of money that wouldn't even buy a stick of gum back in their own countries.

The bar, two blocks from the beach, was full of elderly tourists, mostly in their seventies, and young mulatos from the neighborhood. They sat around little plywood tables and drank Brugal and Coca-Cola, their attention fixed on the host

up on the small concrete stage greeting the audience. He wore a Lycra T-shirt, under which his bulging muscles looked like fluorescent sausages.

"Señoras y señores, signore e signori, ladies and gentlemen, mesdames et messieurs, meine Damen und Herren, willkommen, benvenuti, welcome to tonight's show at One-Eyed Willy's, where your dreams come true. Opening this great evening of fun, I introduce you to Sosúa's very own: El Asco!" And immediately a drag queen appeared on stage who had obviously undergone all kinds of homemade experiments to achieve her womanly curves. The Crisol oil injections had completely deformed her, creating strange bubbles in all the wrong places, and the tight silver muslin dress added a bone-chilling touch to her gray and cadaveric skin. Donna Summer's "I Feel Love" came thundering out of the towers of speakers on either side of the stage, pumping the synthesizers that the electro genius Giorgio Moroder had inaugurated the future with in 1977. Even in Stephan's office, behind the bar, the song's chorus could be heard vibrating, rallying the audience that whistled and clapped to El Asco's deathly sensuality as she mimicked Summers: "looooove."

"Where did you dig up this doll?" asked the German with a strong accent and then, laughing: "You're going to do fine: in this country being white is a profession." Thirty years in the future, Acilde wrote Stephan's complete name in the search engine and saw how, thanks to the popularity of that little bar and its drag show, he had become a well-known impresario with restaurants all over the north coast. Acilde hadn't thought about the cost of the fake IDs and he made a mental note, next to the other mental notes of all the other favors Nenuco had done for him, to pay him back the hundred dollars he was now pulling from his pocket to buy the documents. As Stephan took his photo in front of a

white sheet hung on the door, he asked Acilde what name he wanted on the papers. In the bar, the song was coming to a close and the audience was clapping wildly. "Giorgio," said Acilde, and then added the surname his mother had seen on his father's ID when he'd opened his wallet to pay her: "Giorgio Menicucci."

CÔTE DE FER

A piece of blood sausage drops into each of the wooden bowls held by Roque's men. He has cooked the meal himself to celebrate the sale of the seventy skins they'd had ready when the English returned to Playa Bo. This delicacy is made with wild pig intestines marinated in a Jamaican pepper Captain Ball had brought back from Cuba. Roque is a good cook and he tells Argenis that was how he had made a living on the Spanish galleon that brought him from the Canary Islands. Where there are cattle, there is work. They slaughter and gut the cows so they will always have something to offer the ships that stop on the coast, without which there would be no wine, no oil, no wheat, no gunpowder, nor the pieces of gold and silver accumulating in the chests in which each one of the men also keeps his dreams. Engombe's dream is to be captain of his own ship. The French pirate who he'd been indentured to abandoned him on the north coast with a bucket of water because he had killed a fellow crew member by hitting him on the head with a hammer. The little French guy's: to go back to his homeland and marry a neighbor of his with enormous breasts for whom he's been beating his meat to death. The one-armed man is happy and eating better and more frequently here than in the English dungeon where he was recruited. The Taíno does not have

a treasure chest and wine makes him ill; his dreams are of a sacred geometry that charts the earth from its first days, where a legion of ancestors calls his name.

They've sacrificed two dozen cattle and Roque gives each man a bottle to accompany supper. They eat in peace and snap their fingers to the rhythm of the crickets in the background until Engombe gets up to get another piece of cassava and the little French guy, playfully, sticks his hand in the black man's dish to steal his leftovers. Before he can even touch them, Engombe slices his head off with a scimitar. The head rolls until it stops at Argenis' feet, who sees it blink several times, as if it had something in its eye, and then go completely still. In an extraordinary rage, Argenis knocks Engombe down with a single punch to the chest. Argenis cries with grief over the poor French guy and the one-armed man curses and the Taíno drops to his knees and screams. They all jump on the murderer, and manage to immobilize him and tie him to the base of a guayacán tree. Roque grabs the severed head by the hair and puts it next to Engombe so he'll have to look at it all night long. Argenis cries inconsolably, repeating "Côte de Fer, Côte de Fer," just like the poor innocent man used to do. Giorgio and Iván made Nenuco break down Argenis' studio door to wake him up; his screams could be heard all the way to the house.

For weeks, Argenis had been sleeping during the day and painting at night. He would get up almost always around ten in the evening, his head down and with no appetite. What he was painting, however, had Giorgio very enthused. He'd go see him in his studio with a bag of pot, a bottle of vodka, and a gallon of grapefruit juice. Malagueta would frequently accompany them. Elizabeth was beyond painting, or at the very least it didn't interest her very much, although every now and again she'd come to Argenis' studio with Iván and

they would play music and talk. Argenis would paint on the unstretched canvas on the floor, in a silence broken only by the extraordinarily strange theories he'd spout in response to the simplest questions. Giorgio would ask him things just to see what he would come up with, winking at Elizabeth, who'd make faces and laugh behind his back while playing "Silence is Sexy" by Einstürzende Neubauten, "Traigo de todo" by Ismael Rivera, "Contacto espacial con el tercer sexo" by Sukia, "The Bells" by Lou Reed, "Into the Sun" by Sean Lennon, "Killing Puritans" by Armand Van Helden, "Remain in Light" by Talking Heads, or "Superimposition" by Eddie Palmieri. Whenever Elizabeth opened her mouth, it was to comment on something she'd seen in a magazine or the internet, or to criticize the work of the other local artists who weren't present – these she categorized as black holes, stuck, mediocre, zeros. Argenis knew she had him in that category too, and while he painted he'd make a few interesting efforts to pull himself out of that grouping.

At some point, after she had abandoned one of the three careers her daddy had paid for before art school at Altos de Chavón (sound engineering, creative writing, and cosmetology), Elizabeth had read the *Fluxus Manifesto* in a classmate's scrapbook. Afterward, she'd ordered a bunch of books on conceptual art and various digital cameras from Amazon and she'd declared herself a video artist. She created a series called *Seco y latigoso*, which was, basically, nine loops of scenes of prostitutes working the streets in different zones in Santo Domingo. She'd put them up on the Web on a site with the same name and had managed to get a French curator to include her in a textbook on Third World Contemporary Art. Since then, the whole world kissed her ass. Because of that, and because she had a BMW, a house in Las Terrenas, all the music in the world, and the best pills in the Caribbean. She

had no need to be in the Sosúa Project, but she was there because she felt like it and because, of all of them, she was the only one who was really friends with the Menicuccis.

One day the power went out, but they lit candles and Argenis kept painting. "Monsieur, what do you think about the energy crisis our country has been suffering from for the past thirty years?" Giorgio asked, elbowing Malagueta so he'd pay attention. "In the Caribbean we live on the dark side of the planetary brain, just like with LSD; the neurons that correspond to our islands are very rarely lit, but when they are . . ." responded Argenis as he poured his glass of ice and grapefruit juice onto the canvas to create a watery effect.

Needless to say, the night of the screaming there was no painting party. After waking Argenis, Giorgio brought him a glass of water and, without turning on the light, Iván sat on the bed and told them with that kind of screaming while sleeping the souls of the dead were always involved. "Each person has a spiritual guide, a soul who guides them, a light that helps them; there are also very dark spirits who want to take advantage of you and play tricks and pretend to be good."

Nenuco interrupted. "There was one in Don Frank's house. I work in Don Frank's garden and they found a jug full of gold coins. Now he never has to work again. And you know how he found it? There was an ant invasion in the house and every night he dreamt a black man would eat them. One day he comes to me and says, 'Let me hose them down with hot water to kill them.' He goes to the yard and says, 'Nenuco, help me.' We take a shovel to unearth the ant tunnels and we hit something hard and it was an earthenware jug. There used to be a lot of pirates and runaway slaves who would bury their money around here."

Awake, Argenis kept crying. He felt the true weight of the expectations his talent had generated and felt certain

he would never meet them. The experience he was having with the buccaneers was exhausting. Plus, he had to make something some future collector would want to pay thousands of dollars for, something with a seductive power that would stand the test of time. Lulled by Nenuco's soft singing while Giorgio leaned on the doorframe and looked at him worriedly, he thought about Francis Bacon and Lucian Freud, and about Yeyo, and that if he had been born three hundred years earlier, his technique would have opened doors to the courts of kings. He hated Professor Herman and the pretensions he had picked up from her. I have to get committed to an insane asylum or become an evangelical, he thought, wishing for a relief that neither painting nor the comforts of Playa Bo had brought him.

He was awake at night in two worlds but trying to close the door to the one with the severed head. Giorgio took his hand and Argenis squeezed it as if he were afraid he would fall off a cliff. When he let go, Giorgio pulled his away and lightly touched the palm of his hand. With all eyes closed, Argenis feels as though another body is getting into his bed, cradling and rocking him. A hand caresses his belly, which tenses, then squeezes his glutes. He guesses the route the hand will take and he lets it happen. He has been waiting centuries to be sucked like this, by lips that pull evenly, with a soft and agile tongue, for someone who swallows without fear of gagging on his big dick and who covers his chest and legs with a mantle of long hair that smells of salt and pepper. He forgets about the little French guy, about art, and Playa Bo, he forgets his own name and that of the organ around which the concentric universe now turns. He comes hard, as though emptying his balls forever. He opens his eyes, anesthetized, and sees Roque finally lift his head and throw himself at his side on the cot, snoring almost immediately.

Back in the present, Nenuco, Iván, and Giorgio had gone, leaving him disheveled and alone, with the door to his studio broken and open to the world.

Accompanied by an anecdote about the state of Cuban hospitals and how easy it was to get prescription drugs on the black market, Iván had given Argenis a strip of Valium, thanks to which he was now spending more time in seventeenth-century Sosúa. Either they didn't miss him at the curatorial sessions or his paintings had exonerated him from having to attend. After many days and nights torturing Engombe to make him pay for his crime, Roque has set him free because he needs him to work and fire the arquebus. But Argenis doesn't take his eyes off him, waiting for an excuse to hit him on the head with a rock. After what happened in the cot, he feels disoriented and happy, protected by time, because for him, that past he still didn't recognize as totally his had no repercussions in the present, where he was still a true macho and where no one knew anything. Now he had more reason not to talk about what was happening to him and to keep using the excuse of being the crazy artist to do whatever he wanted with his time. He wants to protect Roque, he wants to impress him. He asks permission to use the press to try and make some engravings and shows the buccaneer a portrait of him he'd carved on an old plank. Roque lets him use the tools that came with the press, which is now in the little hut built by the one-armed man and the dead French guy, thinking that if the engravings are good they could sell some to the smugglers. The first seven hang on the wall with rough nails. Lacking ink, Argenis uses cow's blood, running from the slaughtering with a bucket and applying it immediately, before it can coagulate.

In the first engraving, a black man armed with an arquebus points it at some cattle in the distance. In the second,

a bearded one-armed man is carrying the trunk of a palm tree over the shoulder of his good arm, helped by the little French guy, who Argenis has drawn from memory. He has gone all out to capture the folds of the fabric of their pants, of the linen shirts they all wear, and he's made the one-armed man's Danish clay pipe bigger; he smokes that pipe as much when he works as when he's resting. The third engraving is of a tropical jungle in which a man with a triangular back, his hair in a bun, raises a saber over his head to cut a path through the thicket. The fourth is of the Taíno squatting and stirring the fire on a grill where meat is smoking. In the fifth, Roque poses with an arquebus on his shoulder over the cliff at Playa Bo, wearing a crimson felt hat and two pistols on his belt. The sixth shows Engombe tied to a tree. They'll think he's a slave, thinks Argenis, who signs the engravings "Côte de Fer." The final engraving illustrates the inside of their hut and the clay pot where they keep fresh water in the corner. Under a window, Argenis has captured where his savior sleeps.

The seven plates all come from the same caoba tree. Despite his disability, the one-armed man is very skilled with wood and, following Roque's orders, helps Argenis prepare the plates. The idea of making engravings came to him one evening on the way back from a slaughter. Roque, whose boots were dirty with blood, was leaving red footprints with each step on the rocks to the stream where they'd gone to drink and bathe. His wet curls caressed the muscular definition of his back, which ended in an almost feminine waist. When he turns, Argenis continues carving with his gaze the hairy pelvis that hides a small and relaxed penis and, further up, a brown beard full of even more curls that end at the base of his neck, and from which hangs a copper key on a braided leather necklace.

As he prepares other plates, while the others gut animals or cure skins, Roque lets him stay behind with the Taíno, who marvels at the magical images Côte de Fer produces using just cow blood and caoba. By the glow of the fire they light each night, Argenis gouges the remaining wood with a drawing of Engombe and Roque skinning a cow when he hears screaming. It's coming from the present. This time the screams weren't his but Linda's, who'd come back from the city and her meetings with the Minister of Natural Resources. Stunned, Argenis rushed over and, as he neared the house, he could clearly hear Linda's diatribe: complaining that Playa Bo had become a mess of lazy good-for-nothings eating and drinking, consuming money they could be using to build a lab, the real reason for all this in the first place. "Or did you forget?" she asked. And then he heard Giorgio's voice trying to calm her down, telling her to wait and see what Argenis had produced. "They're treasures," he said. "They will sell for sure."

Giorgio's carefully phrased whispers, as though he were afraid Linda would hit him, made Argenis want to kill her. In his head, Giorgio was an altruistic man who believed in him and she was a conceited and selfish slut. He fantasized about raping and strangling her, then about beating her head in with the aluminum baseball bat Malagueta kept in his studio. Fucking cocksucker. He waited in the dark until the argument was over and imagined Giorgio would come out to give himself a break from the white Jew, giving Argenis the opportunity he so wanted to counsel him, to gratefully be a friend to him, to put his arm around him and let his chest finally touch his patron's. But what he heard instead, after a brief silence, were the whimpers of pleasure from a moist and hasty reconciliation between the Menicuccis. He remained crouched among the dwarf palms until they were

whispering sweet nothings to one another in English and Italian, making the return to his studio so bitter he could feel it in his bones.

He threw himself onto his bed. He stared at the ceiling fan, its blades covered with dust. In his other night, he walks feverishly to the hut with the printing press, where by candle-light he carves, one by one, the plates the one-armed man has prepared for him. He attacks the wood with the same vehemence, insomnia, and alienation he feels attacking him. At dawn he covers the plates with canvas and contemplates the loneliness of the landscape surrounding him, neither prosperous nor cozy, the border between the beach and the forest at the mercy of a lethal attack from a Spanish crew that could arrive, noiselessly, at any moment to cut off their heads, unless a drunk among their own did it first. Why did he have to see this? Who had put him in this place? He remembers the gardener's words and he knows the men with whom he lives and works died a long time ago and that he was wasting his time chasing a beautiful bearded man while carving engravings no one would ever see. Later, in both his bodies, that of Argenis and of Côte de Fer, he went to the beach muttering, "Faggot, loco, crazy faggot," and those words cut him inside with a sharpness like the edges of the reef in whose nooks and crannies he recognized the broad nose and thick lips of his father's profile as if in a paranoid painting by Dalí.

At breakfast, Linda sat on her husband's lap while he brought morsels of fruit salad to her mouth with a little fork. A FedEx truck struggled on the gravel path from the street to the house and they all got up and watched Elizabeth sign some papers and announce, as she opened boxes with a kitchen knife, that her project would be taking a new direction. She pulled out Technics 1200 turntables, a mixer,

and about twenty vinyl records: goodbye video art, hello DJ Elizabeth Méndez.

Iván was radiant with his student's malleability and raised his mimosa in a toast to her future. He'd been pushing her in this direction from the moment he'd heard the music she produced for her videos, which was much more interesting and complex than the images it accompanied. Malagueta proposed that for the presentation of their Goya projects, on which they'd been working for more than a month, they should throw a party, and that it should serve as Elizabeth's debut. In the meantime, Argenis, gutting his fourth animal of the day, froze a hollow smile at the table on the terrace, watching as his paintings shrank before all the shiny silver electronic paraphernalia. Victim to a deep drop in his self-esteem, he felt nauseous and a criminal self-pity. His dreadlocks hung like rotten strings of garlic and the bags under his eyes looked like two used tea bags. "Miss Méndez," he said sarcastically to Elizabeth, "you're a woman of many talents." She lifted her gaze from her new toys for just a second and, without a word, looked him in the eye for the first time in her life. Keen to blow away the black cloud Argenis had once more created with his obvious personality problems, Linda spoke in a voice she hoped would sound concerned: "Argenis, you should see a doctor," she said. "Man, you look like shit."

LAMENTATIONS

Where others saw scenery, Linda Goldman saw desolation. Where others heard relaxing subaquatic silence, she heard the shrieks of life disappearing. Where others saw a gift from God, given for the enjoyment of humankind, she saw an ecosystem fallen victim to a systematic and criminal attack. When she looked at the coral reef, she felt like an oncologist standing before her patient's body. She knew she could save it, although she also understood the disproportionate capacity of evil and its reach down to its finest detail. In order to make the miracle happen, it was necessary to have a measure of extreme optimism and critical realism that would drive anybody crazy. In the reef's case, it wasn't just up to Linda and her team. Salvation depended on re-educating an entire community, and on the government and its long-term protection plan. It was work that would require years, and she'd sworn her life to it. There were days she felt her commitment was irrelevant, when confronted, for example, with a local fisherman's anchor that, in a single minute, had torn a reef hundreds of years old, destroying a valuable specimen and the fish habitat the very same fisherman needed to subsist. The guards charged with enforcing environmental laws in the Cove of Sosúa were the first to ignore them: throwing garbage, fishing with harpoons, and stealing coral to sell – they lacked

a comprehensive education and adequate salaries. For their part, the fishermen had enough problems finding anything to fish to listen to those telling them where and how often they could fish.

Urgency and danger ran through her veins, they were the reason she had been brought up by this sea. In 1939, her father arrived from Austria with his parents. Back then, Sosúa was a jungle, the abandoned lands of the United Fruit Company. There, with 800 other Jews who'd managed to avoid being exterminated, they built a dairy that soon fed the entire country. As a child, she'd spent her free time collecting shells, rocks, and coral at the beach. She'd classify them by shape and color back at the gazebo in her yard. During a trip to New York, her father, Saúl, took Linda and her brothers to the Museum of Natural History. She told her father she wanted to see live animals, not dead ones filled with cotton and formaldehyde. Watching Jacques Cousteau documentaries on local TV, she came to an understanding of the tragedy evolving right under their noses. The sea had been pillaged for centuries and it would soon be empty and sterile. In college, as she worked on her thesis about coral reef diseases in the Caribbean, she went a whole week without sleep. Her friends found her at daybreak, walking naked around campus and carrying a flashlight. After attending her graduation jacked up on pills, she returned to Puerto Plata with a conservation plan her father rejected and with a diagnosis of bipolar disorder.

When Giorgio first laid eyes on her, he was attracted to her spirited ways and her confidence, which he at first mistook for a byproduct of her parents' money. All the men in Cabarete, Sosúa, Playa Dorada, and Playa Cofresí had tried to hit on her without success. Stung by her rejection, some of them had started a rumor that she was a lesbian, when

in fact she just had no time for anybody. She gave wind-surfing lessons during the day. At night, she wrote letters and proposals, trying to get international organizations to carry out preliminary investigations on which she would be able to base her conservation project. She relied on scientific articles that became increasingly more pessimistic about the reefs in the Caribbean, illustrated with photographs that showed white patches gaining more and more territory on the hard but fragile coral. Refusing to use medication, she managed her moods on her own. She'd dive into deep depressions, shutting herself up in her studio and eating only Chef Boyardee straight from the can, convinced the end of the world was irreversible and widespread ignorance would continue to prevent her from saving the ocean. Her older brother would come and dig her out of her hole, stick her in the shower, and give her the money Linda had sworn never to ask for from her father; he'd tell her not to abandon her dreams, that the world needed people like her, and other ready-made self-help phrases that had proven effective over time. When at the end of this therapy Adam would ask her to come work at the dairy for a while, she'd kick him out with enough fury to fill her with energy for days, and that would get her back on track with a kind of manic focus on her embryonic project: a compulsive search for grants and the messianic hope that had led her to fall in love with Giorgio Menicucci.

In the last few years, thanks to 500 daily milligrams of Seroquel and her husband's luck with business, plus an inheritance, they'd been able to buy a parcel of beach and Linda was no longer a human yo-yo. The meds made it possible for her to do her work without euphoria and tragedy, but not a day went by when the vision that had been haunting her since her youth did not stop her dead in her tracks

with anguish: she'd descend to the bottom of a cold and dark sea where the heavy, industrial net of a commercial fishing ship would destroy everything in its path without mercy. In the Gulf of Mexico she'd seen with her own eyes what the nets brought up after shaving the marine floor for miles at a time. Once they had removed everything useful, they'd toss thousands of dead fish too small to be consumed, dolphins, tortoises, and enough coral to build a castle back into the sea, all products of the demolition of an ecosystem that had no resources left to regenerate. She knew how many times these nets were tossed into the waters and she lived each day working against that sinister clock.

Giorgio, on the other hand, hadn't planned on falling in love. His life on the north coast at the end of the twentieth century was going along just fine. He had what he'd always wanted: the body of a man and his own business, a chic pizzeria on a beautiful beach. The mission for which he'd been created had begun to appear on the horizon, but still hadn't indicated a path for him to follow. Linda had left him a note at the restaurant: "Giorgio, I left my windsurfing boards in your alley. Hope it's OK! Linda." He liked that she felt comfortable enough to do that and the next day, when he saw her come in in her cobalt blue wetsuit, he invited her to lunch. He already knew just about everything about Linda: that she was a marine biologist, obsessive and temperamental, that her parents were filthy rich, and that she'd inherit that money even though she was the black sheep of the family. It took her about twenty minutes to feel relaxed enough to open her backpack and pull out a folder full of photos of dying coral, stained and deformed like cancerous livers in a brochure for Alcoholics Anonymous. The folder was worn in a way that gave away how often it was handled. When he saw the source of Linda's anxieties under that pink plastic,

his chest tightened and he felt an urgent need to help her solve all her problems.

In the same way he used to use the PriceSpy, Acilde now used the computer in his cell to look up words or names he didn't recognize when they came up in conversation, or to confirm the assertions of a future business partner. Confronted with Linda's interests, he typed the word coral into the search engine and a site listing all the coral reefs that had disappeared in the tsunami of 2024 popped up on the screen. Giorgio was then able to talk to her about her favorite ones using their names, *Diploria labyrinthiformis* and *Millepora alcicornis*, as though he'd been a fan his whole life. Thanks to this he ended up fucking her right on the shore of Playa Bo that very afternoon. And when she came, she screamed as though she were being murdered.

THE SHADOW OF DAYS

A blond boy in a loincloth waits on a blue beach, spear in his hand, for the fish he'll pierce with it. The sky is the same color as the water.

The movie is *Blue Lagoon* and it's being screened in the dining room of La Victoria prison, while the inmates swallow their portions of synthetic protein and water. It's summer. A row of industrial ceiling fans is useless against the temperature, forty-six degrees Celsius in the shade. Movies in which the sea is full of fish and humans run in bare skin under the sun are now part of the required programming during this season, just like movies about Christ during Holy Week.

"Isn't that something, that now that the sea's dead, that's when they come round to believing in its power?" says an old man with a Cuban accent. He cleans one of his teeth with a toothpick while he makes his way to the trashcan, where he tosses the yellow tray that had carried his lunch. The old man throws the toothpick as though he were shooting a basketball and misses. "In a few years, when those of us who saw it are no longer around, people will talk about the fish in the sea as though they were unicorns," he says as he bends to pick up the toothpick and throw it away.

"Do you want to get some air?" Acilde asked him. He was the only person in the entire prison with his own AC, a little

103

Samsung Mini. Only 12,000 BTUs, it was small enough to fit in a shoebox, which is how the agent who visited him once a month had brought it to him. The agent pretended to be a cousin who brought him groceries, which always included a jar of Peter Pan peanut butter with a message from President Bona buried inside.

"Dude, turn on that air," the old man said, stepping into Acilde's cell. He patted down his bald head with a handkerchief. After aiming the vents so they'd blow in the old Cuban's face (who was panting so hard he seemed on the verge of a heart attack), Acilde opened a small rusty fridge and brought out two mini-bottles of vodka, like the kind they give out on planes, and a can of grapefruit juice. Acilde had met Iván de la Barra a few days after arriving at La Victoria. He had been imprisoned for selling fake Lydia Cabrera and Alejo Carpentier manuscripts, among many other things he'd falsified. As curator of the Havana Biennale, he'd helped launch the careers of several stars of late twentieth-century contemporary art. But as he got older, he'd been marginalized and had survived by selling documents and art, both real and fake, to Latin America's communist oligarchy.

Acilde would kill time with old Iván looking for photos and articles on the computer; he loved the ease with which the ex-curator combined gossip and critical theory in his anecdotes. In one of their conversations, Iván had confessed he'd been receiving messages since he was young from a spirit to whom he owed everything; the dead soul would even advise him on which artists to back and which to avoid. He'd gone against his counsel when, desperate, he'd falsified a draft of a supposedly unpublished manuscript by Lydia Cabrera, titled *Olokun*. "And look how badly things turned out," he said, apologetically. Although he had no religious affiliation, Iván de la Barra may as well have been a PhD when it came

to Afro-Cuban cults. "I got the idea for the book when a collector in Miami showed me a letter from Lydia Cabrera to Pierre Verger; in this letter she recounts how she had managed, finally, to have a conversation with an old woman in Matanzas about the cult of Olokun, the most mysterious of the orishas, about whom even her most cooperative sources had kept quiet. According to the letter, black Cubans called a certain marine creature Olokun. It could travel back in time, dude, very Lovecraftian. First I thought about writing a novel, but the idea of writing a book by a dead person seemed much more interesting."

Iván de la Barra and Acilde gulped down their first drinks in silence. That eased the heat inside and let the vodka calm their senses. Acilde knew the old man liked to watch the official channel and he immediately went to the website to make him happy. "Stalinist remnants," Iván said, excusing his taste, enjoying the chill as the AC touched the wet sweat stains on the armpits of his shirt. On the screen, Said Bona was paying homage to *The Inactives*, an artists' collective that had transformed the Dominican cultural panorama in the 2000s. The president was emotional as he handed plaques to those who, buried in poverty and alcoholism, had survived the disdain of the very same institutions that now offered them paper glory.

Through Iván, Acilde had come to understand that an artist's success is a combination of public relations, a bit of talent, and an extremely well-developed sense of opportunism, or rather, as Iván put it, "the spirit," which had a voice with a slightly different timbre than his own and would tell him "go," "don't go," "say this, say that," "wear the Marc Jacobs jacket," "Cartier is better than Rolex," "lie," "smile," "play it crazy."

It was precisely as Acilde watched the pathetic little group the president was celebrating that the bulb lit up. As Giorgio,

he'd contact the younger Iván de la Barra to "discover" and "promote" the careers of various Dominican visual artists with whom they'd make a mint through their own art gallery. He'd find obscure local talents in their youth, like Argenis Luna who, now decrepit at sixty years of age, was shaking hands with the president on the computer screen. The project would kill several birds with one stone, especially now that he understood the mission for which he was destined was already aligned with his wife's mission. With the money made by the art gallery they'd finally be able to make Linda's dream come true: to build a laboratory at Playa Bo, equipped with all the latest technology, where they'd study and cultivate coral to replant it, whenever it was necessary, in its natural habitat.

ANGELITOS NEGROS

The wind from a fat storm cloud ruffled the trees. Toward the south, a fine black line coagulated on the horizon, which began to dissolve when the raindrops, falling like corn kernels from a sack, stirred a smell of steel, rot, and wood. A drenched Roque ran toward them, shouting: "There's-a-crew-of-Spaniards-coming!" Before he reached the front of the hut where the new skins were treated, Engombe tied the ones that were ready and screamed and pushed the others to do the same. Argenis just had his engravings; he'd packed them in a leather envelope inside Roque's chest to protect them from the salt wind. A few minutes later, carrying the hammocks, the skins, the guns and the tools, some vegetables, and what few belongings they each had, the four men left in Roque's crew walked west, looking for the mangroves along the Sosúa river, which the Taíno knew like the back of his hand and where, according to him, they'd be safe until after the Spaniards had burned down their settlement and returned to Santiago, from where they'd most likely come. The Spanish crew consisted of twenty-five men, who Roque counted as he watched them through the telescope. They were coming down the mountain range and would take them at least another day to reach them. It was imperative to bury the chests and the skins to lighten their load. They stopped

at the foot of a ceiba tree. The winds were dying down and they dug several holes forty feet from the tree. If any of them were to lose their life, the one-armed man reminded them as he dug dirt out of the earth, his chest would be divided among the survivors. They sealed the pact with a drink of water and got back on the move.

When they arrived at the mangrove swamp, it took them hours to light a fire because the rain, which they hadn't seen in months, had made the air heavy and humid. The one-armed man devised a cover to protect the fire, using palm leaves braided with the tangle from the thicket. He stretched the two skins they hadn't buried over the flimsy hideout, with the hope of being able to get some rest – a hope that was quickly dashed when a cloud of mosquitos and gnats invaded, as soon as they were still, and which swelled after Roque ordered them to put out the fire so the smoke wouldn't give them away.

They ate pineapple. They took sips of moonshine. When night fell, an animal moving among the dead leaves kept them awake. At daybreak, with their nerves on edge, they made their way downriver. They were looking for the thickest jungle, least accessible to those on their trail. Argenis cut his big toe and wanted to pause to take a look at his wound. Engombe hit him in the ribs with the butt of the gun to keep him moving. Roque did nothing to stop him. Limping, with his eyes blurred by rheum and bug bites up his ass, Argenis was like a teenager, desperate for Roque's approval; he offered to help him with his burden, talking to him about absurd things in the midst of the heat and the sandy mud that trapped them up to their knees with each step. They stopped before they'd planned to and without any pretense of comfort, resting their heads against rocks or stumps, faint from insects whose attacks did not respect noses, eyes, or mouths. The one-armed man shivered with

cold under the midday sun, his skin festering with pus-filled bites. Engombe covered his arms with wet sand to no avail, cursing the Taíno, whose skin, for whatever reason, was impervious to the pests.

Hostage to a slew of invisible evils in the Playa Bo of 2001, Argenis dragged himself like a penitent from the shower to his bed; he could feel all the stings his buccaneer self was experiencing. Free of any visible wounds, Argenis Luna, participant in the Sosúa Project, overflowed with venom and, to the strain of his throbbing, irritated flesh, he'd found a way to pay back Linda Goldman for the humiliation she'd caused him in front of everyone on the terrace a few days ago.

In a few minutes, the sun would rise and Linda, who never missed her morning walk with her dog, would find the animal hard as rock next to a bush on their property, victim of a nice chunk of Tres Pasitos sausage.

Just like in a cowboy movie, thought Argenis, and then he brushed his skin so he wouldn't have to listen to Linda, who shouted Billy's name once, twice, then many times until one last shapeless shriek let him know that finally she'd found the poor dog on the stairs to the terrace, his jaw stuck in some horrible rictus. Argenis went out, feigning interest, and joined the group surrounding the dog's body at the feet of its masters, who wept inconsolably and held each other. Malagueta, what an ass-kisser, thought Argenis when he saw he too was weeping next to Elizabeth. Though no one knew her to express her feelings, it was obvious she was struggling to project concern and empathy as she squeezed Linda's shoulder.

The day before, during the only walk he'd ever been known to take since arriving at Playa Bo, Argenis had been careful to buy the rat poison and sausage at a food store in another town. He felt like a genius for the first time in years. On the

way he thought of Mirta, his ex, and the possibility of doing the same thing to her, but unfortunately Mirta didn't like sausage. They buried the dear mascot in front of the terrace where he'd interrupted so many conversations, putting his paws on Linda's lap with a tennis ball in his mouth so she would throw it for him, into the darkness, from where he would bring it swiftly back, satisfied and happy. Malagueta went to the trouble of finding a piece of white rock about two feet tall and they placed it like a tombstone over the grave. Iván really stretched his talent for analogy and talked about the death of Mozart, about the damned rainstorm that kept the masses from accompanying the musical genius to the cemetery, about his burial in a secondhand coffin trailed by a handful of folks.

The next day, Giorgio was on his way to supervise the remodeling at the art gallery in the city when he stopped by Argenis' studio because Malagueta was there. He asked him to please sleep in the house and take care of Linda; he didn't even glance at Argenis, who was now a good-for-nothing in his eyes. As far as Giorgio was concerned, Argenis had come to eat his food and lose his mind. As he listened to Giorgio give Malagueta Nenuco's number and instructions about what kinds of tea Linda liked, Argenis caught sight of the canvases he hadn't touched in days, the paint dried on the used brushes which he'd neglected to clean because he'd been busy giving sips of water to a one-armed buccaneer who was shitting all over himself in the infernal swamp in his continuous and exhausting other life.

Malagueta was wearing new Kenneth Cole loafers and a pair of white cotton Bermuda shorts that emulated Giorgio's style to perfection. It had been days since he'd worn his Dodgers cap, and he'd recently gotten back the six-pack buried under the old pot belly, thanks to a regimen of ab exercises.

This guy's cleaning up, thought Argenis, very aware of his own decrepit appearance since Linda had pointed it out at the table.

The 4/4 beat of an electronic bombo was making the studio vibrate. Elizabeth was rehearsing her DJ set for the party they were having that weekend to present the final products of their first two months of work. The guests – collectors, artists, foreign millionaires, surfers from Cabarete, the usual crowd that went to the few electronic parties on the island, and some bureaucrat from the Department of Culture in Puerto Plata – would enjoy an evening dedicated to Francisco de Goya. The flyer for the event, designed by Elizabeth, featured Malagueta in a wig, wearing an eighteenth-century Spanish suit and striking a pose with the palette, paint, and brushes of the Goya photographed by Vicente López. At the bottom of the flyer, in Garamond font, was the name of the event: *Caprichos*. The white of the wig and the gray of the suit contrasted with the blackness of Malagueta's hands and furrowed brow, which made for both a comic and sinister expression. Malagueta gave Giorgio the finished flyers so he could pass them out in the city. He was very enthusiastic in front of Argenis who, thinking that one of his paintings should have been on the flyer, felt slighted once more.

The first lines of Toña la Negra's version of "Angelitos negros" wafted in from Elizabeth's speakers: "Pintor nacido en mi Tierra . . ." The bolero sample on top of the beginning of Basement Jaxx's "Where's Your Head At?", and the long ooooos and the singer's trumpeting introduced the epic spirit of the sound sleeve the DJ was knitting. The turntables, the mixer, the drum machine, and the samples were all on a table against the wall where Elizabeth had tacked and taped up papers, photos, notes on napkins, clippings from newspapers and magazines, songs, ideas, feelings, and pieces by Goya

accompanied by her various interpretations of them, written on yellow Post-Its with her ugly script in red marker. The mural was a constellation of references, accumulated during two months of work with Iván, all-nighters on the internet, and the compulsive consumption of music she'd submitted to in the last few years. This collection was half of what she'd exhibit tonight, right there in her studio, along with the other half, which was what would make people dance after midnight. Her aural archaeology didn't discriminate between genres. She'd learned from hip hop how to find nuggets of gold in a Rocío Jurado ballad as well as in a song by Bobby Timmons, pieces which, loose and looped, created a new music, divorced from the original sources. She stole, without leaving a trace, whole blocks of songs completely alien to one another, which she'd seamlessly weave with minor chords from the synthesizers, and filled the air with the dark nostalgia of the blues and with Dominican-Haitian gagá, which she loved.

While at Altos de Chavón, Elizabeth had visited friends who lived in La Ceja, a batey near La Romana, where every year during Holy Week, like in all the sugar towns on the island, they celebrated a fertility ritual. Under a canopy of branches, three long drums had kept the beat of an all-encompassing rhythm, unfurling hysteria in the polyphonic horns that sought out a marching movement in everybody's legs and bellies. With the full moon at its zenith, she'd seen the sacred purple of the midnight sky over the sugar plantation and a firmament littered with stars. An old man possessed by Papá Candelo walked on coals toward her, patiently picking one up to light his pipe. When he stood by her side, she felt infused by his presence and discovered, specifically and eloquently, the extreme poverty suffered by Haitian workers, the tragic ties with which this ancient ceremony held on to

the present, the permanency of a kind of slavery that now dressed itself up as paid labor, and the power of a music that lodged deities in human bodies, deities powerful enough to swallow the world.

It had all left a huge mark on her soul. Now, its edges took a more tangible form, in the music she remixed so painstakingly, looking for the danceable and mystical effects of that magic formula. She'd spent years aimlessly wandering from one career or project to another and now, finally, she'd hit the mark; her distinct talents could go the distance. The music for the party, a three-hour mix, would trace the flow line from Toña la Negra to the trance music of Goa, and would mine the threatening shadow path and delirious sweetness with minimal tech, deep house and drum 'n' bass, Afro-Cuban prayers, voice samples from Héctor Lavoe, Martin Luther King Jr., Ed Wood, and Gertrude Stein. As a gift to Linda and Giorgio, who she was to some extent indebted to for helping her discover her true vocation, during the third hour's climax and before leaping from a hammering beat to the cyber-hippie ocean of a repetitive trance, she'd throw in a little of Donna Summer's "I Feel Love" and Jacques Cousteau's voice from the *Haiti: Waters of Sorrow* documentary. The effect would be tragic, inspiring, and contradictory: the French explorer's predictions about the future of the island's marine life would hang in silence for a few seconds until the bass came down again, like a tsunami, over the dance floor.

Argenis' rock-trained ears took a long time to grasp what his colleague had spent several days putting together in her studio. The one-armed man is not getting better. Argenis seems to be the only one trying to take care of him, to wet his forehead with a rag, to listen to his ravings in a rough English he can't understand, moving his stump around as though he still has his arm. Roque stays awake, guarding

their refuge and going on patrols to make sure they're safe. They eat moldy leftover cassava, not daring to light a fire or eat tilapia, which they could easily fish, because at the slightest move Engombe points the pistol at Argenis and the Taíno. The cut on his foot is infected and he tries to stay close to the sick man without moving too much so he won't feel the pain. It causes cramps up his leg, which are not relieved by the aspirins he takes four at a time in the Menicucci complex.

Nobody brought him soups or coffee, or came to talk; his medical leave and the sympathies he might have provoked in others were over and done. Malagueta had done him the favor of opening the studio curtains and reminded him, in case he'd forgotten, that the party was tonight and they expected him to organize his studio and exhibit his pieces. He also offered, though not sincerely, to help him stretch his canvases out on the frames. Through the window he saw when Giorgio returned from the city and that two workers, one with a pick and the other with a shovel, were following him. The one-armed man has died overnight and now leaks all kinds of bodily fluids; they don't know what to do with his corpse, all bruised and stinky. Flying above them in circles and drawn by the smell of death, the vultures will also attract the Spaniards' attention. They decide to move on, to abandon the body to the scavengers to do with as they please. He's curious why he feels sympathy now and not with that fucking Billy.

On a bench in front of the studios, Giorgio pulled a paper from a tube and showed the enthusiastic group the plans for the building that would be Linda's lab, commissioned to the same architect who was doing the art gallery. Linda was surprised and smiled for the first time since the death of her dog. Construction was set to begin at noon, with a

little ceremony that would require everyone's presence; that way the evening's party would still have its own reason for celebration. At the appointed hour, they gathered on the terrace. Linda looked like she'd been crying a lot and gazed at Giorgio with devotion as she talked on her cell to her colleague James Kelly, sharing the good news with him. The group, including Nenuco and Ananí, carried a cooler, a tablecloth, and brown bags with snacks. They surrounded Linda as they walked, made jokes about the future lab and, in their joy, left Argenis behind, who limped and leaned on a broomstick he'd found in the kitchen. The place chosen for the ceremony was a clearing on the other side of the street, acquired for a few cents, right in front of the Menicuccis' property.

A few miles from the place where the vultures are circling, the buccaneers advance uneasily, hesitating over the mangrove roots while below in the muddy stream hundreds of crabs open and shut their pincers. Argenis made a superhuman effort to move his legs in both places, no longer asking himself why this was happening, and follows the others like a zombie.

"A great adventure starts now," said Giorgio as he pulled a bottle of champagne from the cooler. Behind him, the two workers marked the place where the lab would be with four stakes and rope. Malagueta and Iván spread the tablecloth over the dry and yellow grass. Argenis was the first to sit down and the last to receive a glass. They toasted to the Playa Bo Marine Research Center. Iván poured some drops from his glass on the ground and asked for favor from the spirits buried there. Giorgio whistled with both fingers so the workers, who were fanning themselves with their caps, would begin to dig right there, where they would soon lay the foundations. The place was perfect, with access to the main

road and in a small glade with perfect features, surrounded by the shade of almond trees, flame trees, and a ceiba, next to whose roots the picnic was taking place.

Argenis suddenly remembered where Roque had ordered them to bury the chest with his engravings. The Menicuccis' workers drove their tools; they pulled out years of dirt and cow shit from among the ceiba's enormous roots, which had grown like tentacles in the Antillean summers. The pain in Argenis' foot and the rest of his problems abruptly vanished with a sudden burst of adrenaline. Giorgio was caressing his wife's face with the back of his hand; unshaven for several days, an incoming beard darkened his chin. With his other hand, he tipped the bottle with the very same elegance with which the chief of the buccaneers had advanced through the swamp, leaving Argenis alone and at the mercy of the crabs, the heat, and the vultures. They were going to let him die and his engravings would be harvested by pick and shovel by Giorgio and his whore. Argentis turned back, leaping from root to root as though possessed, injuring his foot again on thorns and animals as he searched for the place where they had buried the chest, which he would unearth with his teeth if he needed to.

As they come out of the mangrove swamp, Engombe and Roque turn back for him. They care about me and they've returned to find me, he thought. But as he arrives at the foot of the ceiba four hundred years before everyone gathered for the picnic, he realizes the barrel of Engombe's arquebus is on his neck. Roque puts his hand on the gun, forcing Engombe to lower it just as Giorgio rolled up his sleeves, breathing uncomfortably in the heat. Both look at Argenis with the same eyes, creating a tunnel of silence; on one side, glasses clinked in toasts, on the other, an inexplicable and nauseating truth echoes. "And now what's the matter

with you?" asked Giorgio and Roque in unison. Argenis trembled in panic, unable to open his mouth. "Don't waste the bullet," Roque says to Engombe, as he takes the gun by the barrel and swings it like a bat, striking Argenis and knocking him down with a blow to the head, but not before moving his buccaneer mouth to say: "This is for Billy, you sonuvabitch."

MONKEY MAGIC

Malagueta knew their type: light-skinned mulatos, middle-class, without a dime or lineage to brag shit about, but who thought – because they were born in the city under a cement roof and not a zinc one – that they were better than everybody else. They'd come to his childhood beach and look at him and his little friends as though they were dirty pigeons from the plaza. They'd enjoy the sea and sun, avoiding their dark little bodies as if they were dirt balls obscuring the view. That's why, when he saw Argenis disrupting the picnic with his madness, he couldn't control himself. Giorgio had planned the event to make Linda feel better, and now Argenis had to come and screw it up. The day had been splendid – little tuna sandwiches, the breeze, and the joy in the face of the blonde, as Malagueta called Linda, dreaming about her future laboratory. Suddenly, the workers, who had started to dig a hole for the foundations ahead of the bulldozer's arrival, stumbled onto something and called Giorgio over. He went to see, a look of surprise coming over his face, then called everyone over.

Argenis had spent a half hour staring at the checkered tablecloth when he suddenly stood up and pushed Giorgio. "You're not going to trick me," he said. "This is a sham, you sonuvabitch, you're the devil himself, you cheated me, you all know it, you're part of this, don't pretend, you all did this

together, the stuff you found is mine, it's my treasure, I made them all, look, don't do this to me, please, I don't deserve it." Argenis whimpered and screamed, his eyes orbiting as he kicked when Malagueta put a headlock on him with just one arm and dragged him away, toward the house. Argenis watched through tears and snot as the two workers pulled the chest out of the dirt with Nenuco's help.

Malagueta slapped him twice with his baseball glove-sized hand and then, grabbing him by the collar and the seat of his pants, threw him in the shower. "Have you calmed down now, you goddamn freak?" He left him in a fetal position in the tub and picked up what little stuff he had. He threw away the dirty underwear piled up in a corner of the bathroom. He let him keep the same clothes he'd had on for days, which now, because of the water, smelled of pee and chicken shit. He borrowed Giorgio's van and pushed Argenis inside, driving away and toward the group as it returned from the picnic. The two workers carried a chest turned red from dirt and rust. He honked the horn, pan-para-ran-pán, but without pausing, and got a glimpse of Linda's face, the only one who expressed any kind of worry or embarrassment for the man in the passenger seat.

When they got to the bus stop, Argenis, head down and disoriented, kept bumping into couples kissing goodbye, old ladies buying orange sweets, and smokers on their last puff before climbing the bus. Malagueta didn't say a word to him until he'd sat him next to a woman with two dozen eggs on her lap. "Bro," he said, "they gave you a helluva opportunity and you blew it." He gave him one hundred pesos so he could take a cab to his mother's house once he got to the city, a small bottle of water, and a bag of chips.

On the way back, Malagueta felt a certain lightness in his shoulders and neck. He fired up a Marlboro Light, poked

his left arm out the car window, and steered with the right. He'd just relieved himself of a burden. No one could stand Argenis anymore, no one wanted to take care of him. The dirty work, of course, had fallen on the black guy. "Black," he heard himself say as he breathed smoke out of his mouth. A small word swollen over time by other meanings, all of them hateful. Every time somebody said it to mean poor, dirty, inferior, or criminal, the word grew; it must have been about to burst, and when it finally did, it would once again mean what it meant in the beginning: a color. His body was a vessel containing the word, inflated now and again by the odious stares from those others, the ones who thought they were white. He knew Argenis, curiously the darkest of them all after Malagueta, didn't see it this way, and his condescending look, the same look he used with animals, women, and faggots, hurt him. He imagined Argenis' mind like a table of colors, the kind he used when he bought acrylics; the darker the color, the more disdain. He'd gotten rid of a cocksucker who'd never be able to look himself in the mirror without fear. "Fucking nigger," Malagueta said aloud, thinking of Argenis, and a burst of laughter made him shake; he had to stop the vehicle because he was crying from so much laughing.

Back at Playa Bo, all was curiosity and activity. The catering company was putting together a long table for the appetizers and the bar. With the help of a friend who'd come in from the city, Elizabeth was setting up the sound system, which included a tower of speakers seven feet tall. Giorgio was on his cell, talking about the morning's events, pacing from one side of the terrace to the other, excited, with a nervous rasp in his voice, and trying to pressure whoever was on the other end of the line to come immediately. Inside the house, following Linda's directions, workers moved the modular walls to enlarge the living room where now, as if by magic, there were

two Le Corbusier sofas, retrieved from the warehouse at the rear of the house. Ananí had just finished cleaning what had been Argenis' studio, filling a trash bag with linens, papers, stiffened socks, dried brushes, and cigarette butts. Nenuco rolled Argenis' paintings into tubes; apparently, they would not be exhibited during the evening's activities. When they were ready, they took out the bed and the desk and filled the space with candles, creating a kind of Eden for their guests.

In his room, Malagueta had a mirror he used to look at himself during his exercises and rehearsals. There was a photo of Ana Mendieta blending into the trunk of a tree on the frame; a second showed Pedro Martínez throwing one of the curveballs that won the Boston Red Sox the 1999 playoffs against the Cleveland Indians. Lastly, there was a drawing he'd done when he was nine years old of Goku, from *Dragon Ball*, with his monkey tail. When he was little, every time somebody called him "monkey," or "goddamned monkey," or "the devil's monkey," he'd draw Goku kicking something or using one of his special powers. He'd filled whole notebooks trying to survive the words that would sometimes come out even from his mother's mouth, or his brothers', dreaming that, someday, after he'd found a teacher like Mr. Miyagi or Yoda, he'd acquire powers to beat the enemy, that big dirty mouth that hurt him and made him weak. Lacking a sensei, Malagueta had come up with another way out: the foul air of the insults would swell his muscles, pumping his arms end-lessly with weights and becoming the gorilla no one dared defy – a batting machine. When he got injured and had to set his baseball dreams aside, he had three options: work as a host in a hotel, fuck old European women in exchange for brand-name T-shirts, or both.

The Sosúa Project had saved him. There he'd found his teacher, that skinny Cuban who'd taught him to understand

secret voices, use the invisible power of the history of his body, and plan a strategic attack against the repulsive and cruel mouths on everyone. In two months, Iván had broken down Jung, Foucault, Fanon, and Homi Bhabha without once cracking open a book. The multiple directions Iván's anecdotes took, his jokes, his reflections, his questions, and his reprimands had helped Malagueta discover his body as an instrument with a voice that he could use convincingly and completely, shutting down the repetitive and ignorant shouts of others. For his performance that night, he'd decided to continue using elements from baseball, like Iván had suggested. The accessories of the sport were beautiful and sterile and brought with them a solid current of meaning. For the first time, he'd confront the theme of race and Dominican masculinity head on; he wouldn't be lacking much in the way of props. And, as Iván liked to say, he'd also apply marketing rules to his "show," with an aesthetic proposal designed to satisfy the needs and anxieties of a particular audience who would read it as style instead of fashion, and a search instead of a trend. He'd had bleach in his hair for about an hour now. His Afro was too tight and his skin too dark, so that when he washed out the chemical, his hair was an orange, carrot color instead of Goku Super-Sayayín yellow. Elizabeth came to comb it out for him with a tool for punk styles and told him the orange was even stranger and that it would allude to *Dragon Ball* in a more indirect and interesting way. She was wearing a very tight pair of white pants. Malagueta heard himself say, "If I get my hands on you," in his head, but kept his mouth shut. He looked at himself in the mirror one last time. He'd stopped drinking water two days ago so his muscles would be more defined. Now his skin was pure plastic.

THE WATER STAINS

The news of his upcoming release came, like all the news from the Palace, in a little paper scroll inside a jar of peanut butter. After ten years in La Victoria – comfortable, calm, without any responsibilities other than to eat and breathe – he was now headed to the outside world, where the asphalt would stick to his soles like gum. He'd have to work now, that was certain. How would he deal with his stuff, his other lives, his businesses? He'd begged the president to do whatever it took to let him continue inside, with his little fridge, his friend, his free time. But Bona was sick and tired of waiting for the miracle that, according to Esther Escudero, Acilde was destined to bring forth. For the first time in years, he thought about Peri, Morla, and his life before he'd met Omicunlé. Bona was an idiot and Acilde had no way of explaining that he had access to the past via an extra body that was funding the research that would allow the Caribbean coral reefs to be repopulated in this shitty present.

Although the ceiling of his cell had been painted only a few weeks before, water stains had begun to reappear. In the past the humidity had allowed for the excessive fecundity that nourished the tropical jungle in Sosúa, but in 2037 it was an unbreathable and oppressive aggravation. The water stains had entertained him during nights of insomnia, while

Giorgio and Roque slept. He could make out animal shapes and still lifes. He used them to distract himself during nights in the present that only made sense when dealing with other people in other times.

He got up off the floor where he'd been sleeping to check in on Iván de la Barra. They had been sharing a cell for months. He'd thought the old man, now disoriented and forgetful, would benefit from sleeping in an air-conditioned room. Later, when he saw the effort it took for him to get up off the floor, he'd given him his bed. Sleep, which Iván achieved thanks to pills his sisters sent from Cuba, gave the old man a healthy aspect that wakefulness stole away.

Acilde looked over at his little rusted fridge, at the green light from the hallway that streamed in through the also rusted cell bars, at the plastic rectangle he'd used to cover the door so the cool air wouldn't escape, and at the bucket of water he used to flush the toilet. Now that he'd finally managed to complete almost all his plans, this, his control tower, seemed for the first time like a dirty and pathetic cell.

He waited until the sun rose. He woke Iván, shaking him a little carelessly. "C'mon, old man, get up – I need my bed."

In the hideous interpretation of "Angelitos negros" that was playing, the trumpets seemed to announce the reading of a royal edict at Playa Bo. The guests chatted and held their appetizers on little napkins, all local delicacies prepared in Giorgio's restaurant. Eel sushi and green plantains, pigeon pea and coconut frittata, grouper and passion-fruit brochettes, etc. Nenuco, working as a valet that evening, arranged the cars and made sure the guests entered the property through the proper gate, walking the two hundred meters to the house through a garden filled with crotons, bromeliads, palms, cayenne, lemons, and avocados, at the center of which Malagueta performed his piece for the guests to enjoy. That's why everyone turned to look when an ancient Lincoln Continental drove up to the very lip of the terrace, spitting gravel as it pushed through. From that black submarine emerged a rail-thin man wearing a long-sleeved, cream-colored guayabera and a pair of polyester khakis. He carried a locked portfolio in his right hand, the kind used only by medical suppliers for their samples and papers.

Orlando Kunhardt dug up corpses. He gave life back to objects from other times: archaeologist, anthropologist, restorer. His eyes – trained at UNAM in the seventies – didn't need books, magnifying glasses, or chemicals to determine,

in a minute, the authenticity of a find such as the chest now resting in Giorgio and Linda's room, with the AC going, just as Orlando had recommended over the phone. Once in the room, he pulled on a pair of green latex gloves; outside the room the earth shook with apocalyptic hard techno and he signaled for Giorgio to close the bedroom door. He pulled a piece of hardened mud off the chest. It was possible to see ancient ant tunnels on the chunk of dirt. "It's oak," was the first thing he said as he caressed the chest's bruised wood and felt the bass from the party music resonating through it. He walked around it while lighting up a menthol Nacional. He noticed the chest had a missing hinge. "For the chest alone, I can get you about 12,000 dollars," he said, blinking because smoke had gotten in one of his eyes. "That is, unless you want to donate it," he added, very seriously, as though it was no joke. He knelt to try and force the lock, but sensed his client's impatience. "It's okay, we'll pretend it's a young virgin," he said. Giorgio had already described the discovery to him and Orlando had come prepared. He pulled a ring of antique keys from his portfolio, selected one in an F shape, and inserted it into the lock, which gave instantly. When the chest creaked open, the second hinge fell and the lid came loose; Giorgio had to rush to grab it so it wouldn't fall to the floor. Inside they found a leather envelope, a tortoise shell, and a long braid of brown hair. Orlando lifted the envelope as the cigarette dangled from his lip. He pulled out a handful of thick papers. He thought his eyes were going to pop out. Giorgio pretended to be curious but decided to wait for Dr. Kunhardt's verdict before asking questions. Foreign specialists would confirm his findings later. "Man alive, this is a real treasure," said Kunhardt, not letting go of the Nacional between his lips. The first seven engravings, all signed by a certain Côte de Fer, showed buccaneer life in the seventeenth

century. The technique was impeccable, the documentation of the details of domestic life, invaluable. The other engravings were an erotic series in which a woman, most likely a prostitute, was submitted to the desires of a group of men who joyfully filled all her orifices. The images were extremely graphic and bore some relation to the brutal aesthetic of Goya's *The Disasters of War*. The poses were increasingly more violent until they reached the last one, in which a black man sodomized her while a one-armed man cut off her head with a scimitar. I should have killed him twice, thought Giorgio, who recognized the victim's face as Linda's. He took some pleasure in thinking they would soon find Côte de Fer's skull, shattered by Roque's sharp blow earlier that morning. Orlando was talking about pigments and rust and blood. "This is major league, Giorgio, this guy was a genius." Was, thought Giorgio, and he left the room and let Iván de la Barra go in and conjecture with Orlando, imagining the moment when the engravings were created, trying to smell the smoked meat on the paper, speculating about the school the artist belonged to, making the presumption that he'd come from France, and calculating the possible prices the pieces would sell for at international art auctions. "Imagine, an artist as great as Goya one hundred years earlier in Hispaniola," Giorgio heard the Cuban say.

Everything with Argenis had been an accident. Giorgio hadn't imagined another human could replicate himself in the past the way he did. But maybe more than an accident, it had been a stroke of luck. As he walked through the party, he began to celebrate the final step of what he'd planned that morning when the English smuggler had shown him the press. He'd sell half the engravings to collectors and museums and exhibit the other half in the Casa Museo Côte de Fer, which would be housed on the first floor of the laboratory.

On its outside walls, they'd recreate a buccaneer settlement; the guides would be dressed as pirates (although that might be too much). The government would give them a subsidy and the complex would live off the business from the nearby all-inclusive hotels.

This compulsive optimism was proof the ecstasy he'd taken a half hour earlier was beginning to take effect. Elizabeth had made him close his eyes and open his mouth to swallow the two green pills, the same color green as the Bayer anti-mosquito candles that burned in a spiral.

The first wave of pleasure forced him to sit down. He felt the drug-stimulated serotonin infusing his brain and making everything agreeable, desirable, and possible. Wearing a white halter and pants that were green like the pills, Linda danced in a corner of the terrace with a bottle of water in her hand. Surely she felt like he did. They exchanged a complicit look, like old friends. He loved her. She was his queen. Suddenly, the idea struck him as real: he was a king, the king of this world, the big head, the one who knew what was at the bottom of the sea. Generally speaking, he usually went on his way, not giving too much thought to any of that so he wouldn't go crazy, pulling the strings on Giorgio and Roque from his cell in La Victoria as though he were playing a video game, accumulating goods, trophies, experience, enjoying the view, inexistent in that future of acid rains and epidemics in which prison was preferable to the outside.

Thanks to the establishment of this lab, he thought, Said's government will have something to help regenerate part of what was lost. This lab is the altar I'm going to build for Olokun, in which I'll turn Omicunlé's Yoruba prayers into an environmental call to action. His work was finished. Elizabeth was making the dancers grind out on the floor with the Chemical Brothers' "Out of Control"; a huddle formed in the

center, where something was happening. Giorgio got up to see, proud and happy. He peered between the heads of his guests and saw a young man breakdancing. He was going in circles at a breathtaking speed, posed on the axis of his back while holding a fetal position. In Giorgio's dilated pupils, his figure seemed to become a lotus flower in a cloudscape. Without slowing down, he froze, his elbow on the ground and a fist under his defiant chin while his other hand went to his waist, as if waiting for a photo. It was Said Bona, now twenty-two years old.

The victory odes Giorgio had been singing to himself came to a dead halt. He was terrified. The flashes from the disco ball made everything move in slow motion. Here was the person responsible for the deplorable state of the sea a few decades from now. Here was the reason for his initiation. All that for this. Quickly and overwhelmingly, he had before him the real goal of his mission: to give Said Bona a message – as president, to avoid accepting biological weapons from Venezuela. To tell him that, in the future, when he was elected president, he needed to reject them: Giorgio had to convince him. But just as quickly, he began to think about the other consequences of that decision: if Said Bona followed his advice and there was no chemical spill after the tsunami, would Esther Escudero go looking for him? Would Eric Vitier find him among the hustlers at El Mirador? Would he be crowned in that shanty in Villa Mella and allowed the life he'd come to so appreciate? Would Giorgio disappear? He imagined Linda covering her head with her hands, out of her mind when her seas turned into a shit shake, while here, in the past of those seas destined to disappear, she was dancing happily with the prospect of the new lab next to a young and charming Iván. Giorgio walked toward the cliff. A little group was sitting on the rocks, smoking a blunt

while looking at the stars. In his mind, he reviewed all he'd experienced and accumulated, then sat down among those passing around that giant joint. He felt the intense pulse of his three lives at the same time and the weight of the sacrifice his little game was demanding of him now. The pot had given the ecstasy a second wind. He went back to the house to talk to Said, who was hanging out with Elizabeth behind the turntables. She was clearly enchanted. "This is Said," she said, introducing him. "He's a graffiti artist and does spoken word. And he's great."

"I know who he is," said Giorgio, immediately capturing the attention of the future president, who was all ears when it came to flattery.

SALTPETER

The lion-paw bathtub sat in the center of the circular bathroom, under a meter-wide skylight made from crushed beer bottles and through which the sun came in a soft emerald color. Linda Goldman listened as the last guests drove away. She figured Giorgio must have seen them off. Malagueta, Elizabeth, and Iván continued the rumba at a supposed after-party in some villa in Cabarete. Her house was finally free of everyone; she was free of complaints. She rubbed her body from head to toe with an orange blossom essential oil and put on a terry cloth bathrobe to go out on the terrace and look for her husband. She wandered over to the studios. There she found lizards that ran from her steps and hid noisily among the dry leaves. She walked to the edge of the cliff. Later, she looked out at the beach, to no avail. Hidden behind a sea grape tree, Giorgio listened to her call his name. When Linda got close enough, he grabbed her from behind. He had a gallon of grapefruit juice in his hand and laughed when Linda punched him in the gut as a reaction to his scaring her. He looked for cups, ice, and vodka, but Nenuco and Ananí had already cleared everything away. He found half a bottle in the freezer and made two drinks. They sat on the couch, under the Lam painting.

Giorgio closes his eyes and noisily chews on some ice. He sees the sleeping pills stolen from old Iván and which Acilde is now popping in his mouth. Lost, because the Taíno has snuck away in the night, Roque and Engombe run from the helmeted squad that splashes toward them, getting closer and closer. Acilde swallows the last of the pills with a drink of water from his sink and sits back on his little bed. The weight of his eyelids closes Giorgio's access to the cell in which his original body has lived. He feels that someone very dear to him is dying and discovers tears in his eyes. The squad falls on Roque, who doesn't wipe away the tears and instead lifts the arquebus defiantly to speed up the dénouement. The shot that takes him down leaves Giorgio completely dark inside. After chatting about rap and politics, he'd said goodbye to Said without a word about his future. He could sacrifice everything except this life, Giorgio Menicucci's life, his wife's company, the gallery, the lab. Linda rests her head on his lap and, with a finger, he moves a strand of wet hair that has fallen on her face. In a little while, he'll forget about Acilde, about Roque, even about what lives in a hole down there in the reef.

Dear readers,

As well as relying on bookshop sales, And Other Stories relies on subscriptions from people like you for many of our books, whose stories other publishers often consider too risky to take on.

Our subscribers don't just make the books physically happen. They also help us approach booksellers, because we can demonstrate that our books already have readers and fans. And they give us the security to publish in line with our values, which are collaborative, imaginative and 'shamelessly literary'.

All of our subscribers:

- receive a first-edition copy of each of the books they subscribe to
- are thanked by name at the end of our subscriber-supported books
- receive little extras from us by way of thank you, for example: postcards created by our authors

BECOME A SUBSCRIBER, OR GIVE A SUBSCRIPTION TO A FRIEND

Visit andotherstories.org/subscriptions to help make our books happen. You can subscribe to books we're in the process of making. To purchase books we have already published, we urge you to support your local or favourite bookshop and order directly from them – the often unsung heroes of publishing.

OTHER WAYS TO GET INVOLVED

If you'd like to know about upcoming events and reading groups (our foreign-language reading groups help us choose books to publish, for example) you can:

- join our mailing list at: andotherstories.org
- follow us on Twitter: @andothertweets
- join us on Facebook: facebook.com/AndOtherStoriesBooks
- admire our books on Instagram: @andotherpics
- follow our blog: andotherstories.org/ampersand

This book was made possible thanks to the support of:

Aaron McEnery · Aaron Schneider · Adam Bowman · Adam Lenson · Adelle Stripe · Adriana Diaz Enciso · Aileen-Elizabeth Taylor · Ailsa Peate · Aisling Reina · Ajay Sharma · Alan Donnelly · Alan McMonagle · Alan Simpson · Alana Marquis-Farncombe · Alasdair Hutchison · Alastair Gillespie · Alex Hancock · Alex Ramsey · Alex Robertson · Alexandra Citron · Alexandra Stewart · Alfred Birnbaum · Ali Casey · Ali Conway · Ali Smith · Alice Clarke · Alicia Bishop · Alison Riley · Alison Winston · Alistair McNeil · Alyse Ceirante · Alyssa Tauber · Amado Floresca · Amanda · Amanda Astley · Amanda Silvester · Amber Da · Amelia Ashton · Amelia Dowe · Amine Hamadache · Amitav Hajra · Amy Bojang · Amy Rushton · Ana Savitzky · Anastasia Carver · Andra Dusu · Andrea Reece · Andrew Kerr-Jarrett · Andrew Marston · Andrew McCallum · Andrew Rego · Angela Everitt · Angharad Jones · Ann Moore · Ann Sheasby · Anna-Maria Aurich · Anna Badkhen · Anna Glendenning · Anna Milsom · Anna Pigott · Anne Carus · Anne Frost · Anne Goldsmith · Anne Guest · Anne Stokes · Anneliese O'Malley · Anonymous · Anonymous · Anonymous · Anthony

Quinn · Antonia Lloyd-Jones · Antonio de Swift · Antony Pearce · Aoife Boyd · Archie Davies · Asako Serizawa · Asher Norris · Audrey Mash · Avril Marren · Barbara Black · Barbara Mellor · Barbara Wheatley · Barry John Fletcher · Ben Schofield · Ben Thornton · Benjamin Judge · Bettina Rogerson · Beverly Jackson · Bianca Jackson · Bianca Winter · Briallen Hopper · Brian Anderson · Brian Byrne · Bridget McGeechan · Brigita Ptackova · Caitlin Halpern · Caitlin Liebenberg · Caitriona Lally · Callie Steven · Cam Scott · Carl Emery · Carlos Gonzalez · Carol Christie · Carol Mavor · Carol McKay · Carolina Pineiro · Caroline Bennett · Caroline Haufe · Caroline Mager · Caroline Maldonado · Caroline Picard · Caroline Smith · Caroline Waight · Caroline West · Carolyn Johnson · Cassidy Hughes · Catharine Mee · Catherine Lambert · Catherine Rodden · Catherine Rose · Cathy Czauderna · Catriona Gibbs · Cecilia Rossi · Cecilia Uribe · Cecily Maude · Chantal Wright · Charles Fernyhough · Charles Raby · Charles Dee Mitchell · Charlotte Briggs · Charlotte Holtam · Charlotte Middleton · Charlotte Murrie & Stephen Charles · Charlotte Ryland · Charlotte Whittle · Chia Foon

Yeow · China Miéville · Chris Gostick · Chris Gribble · Chris Lintott · Chris Maguire · Chris McCann · Chris Nielsen · Chris Stevenson · Chris Young · Chris & Kathleen Repper-Day · Christina Moutsou · Christine Dyer · Christine Elliott · Christine Hudnall · Christine Luker · Christopher Allen · Christopher Stout · Ciara Ní Riain · Claire Adams · Claire Brooksby · Claire Malcolm · Claire Riley · Claire Tristram · Claire Williams · Clare Archibald · Clari Marrow · Clarice Borges · Claudia Nannini · Claudio Scotti · Cliona Quigley · Clive Bellingham · Colin Denyer · Colin Matthews · Courtney Lilly · Csilla Toldy · Cyrus Massoudi · Dag Bennett · Dan Raphael · Daniel Arnold · Daniel Coxon · Daniel Gallimore · Daniel Gillespie · Daniel Hahn · Daniel Manning · Daniel Reid · Daniel Sweeney · Daniela Steierberg · Darina Brejtrova · Darius Cuplinskas · Darren Davies · Dave Lander · Davi Rocha · David Anderson · David Hebblethwaite · David Higgins · David Irvine · David Johnson-Davies · David Mantero · David Miller · David Shriver · David Smith · David Steege · David Travis · David F Long · Davis MacMillan · Dean Taucher · Debbie Pinfold · Declan Gardner · Declan O'Driscoll · Deirdre Nic

Mhathuna · Denis Larose · Denis Stillewagt & Anca Fronescu · Diana Digges · Diana Powell · Diana Fox Carney · Dominick Santa Cattarina · Dr. Paul Scott · Duncan Clubb · Duncan Marks · E Rodgers · Eamon Flack · Ed Burness · Ed Tronick · Edward Thornton · Ekaterina Beliakova · Eleanor Dawson · Eleanor Maier · Elhum Shakerifar · Elie Howe · Elina Zicmane · Elisabeth Cook · Eliza O'Toole · Elizabeth Cochrane · Elizabeth Draper · Elizabeth Soydas · Ellen Coopersmith · Ellen Wilkinson · Elliot Marcus · Elvira Kreston-Brody · Emily Bromfield · Emily Taylor · Emily Yaewon Lee & Gregory Limpens · Emma Bielecki · Emma Parker · Emma Perry · Emma Teale · Emma Louise Grove · Enrico Cioni · Erin Cameron Allen · Ewan Tant · F Gary Knapp · Fatima Kried · Filiz Emre-Cooke · Finbarr Farragher · Fiona Liddle · Fiona Quinn · Florence Reynolds · Florian Duijsens · Fran Sanderson · Frances de Pontes Peebles · Francesca Brooks · Francis Mathias · Freda Donoghue · Friederike Knabe · Gabriel Vogt · Gabriela Lucia Garza de Linde · Gabrielle Crockatt · Garan Holcombe · Gary Gorton · Gavin Smith · Gawain Espley · Genaro Palomo Jr · Genia Ogrenchuk · Geoff Thrower · Geoffrey Cohen · Geoffrey Urland · George Christie · George Hawthorne · George McCaig · George Stanbury · George Wilkinson · Georgia Panteli · German Cortez-Hernandez · Gill Adey · Gill Boag-Munroe · Gillian Grant · Gillian Spencer · Gordon Cameron · Graham Fulcher · Graham R Foster · Grant Rintoul · Greg Bowman · Gregory Ford · Guy Haslam · Hadil Balzan · Hamish Russell · Hank Pryor · Hannah Dougherty · Hannah Harford-Wright · Hans Krensler · Hans Lazda · Hayley Newman · Helen Brady · Helen Collins · Helen Conford · Helen Coombes · Helen Waland · Helen Wormald · Henrike Laehnemann · Henry Patino · Hilary McGrath · Howard Robinson · Hugh Gilmore · Hyoung-Won Park · Ian Barnett · Ian Buchan · Ian McMillan · Ian Mond · Íde Corley · Ieva Panavaite & Mariusz Hubski · Ifer Moore · Ines Fernandes · Ingrid Olsen · Irene Mansfield · Irina Tzanova · Isabel Adey · Isabella Livorni · Isabella Weibrecht · Ivona Wolff · J Collins · Jacinta Perez Gavilan Torres · Jack Brown · Jack Fisher · Jacqueline Lademann · Jacqueline Ting Lin · Jacqueline Vint · Jadie Lee · James Beck · James Crossley · James Cubbon · James Kinsley · James Lehmann · James Lesniak · James Mewis · James Portlock · James Purdon · James Scudamore · James Tierney · James Ward · Jamie Cox · Jamie Mollart · Jamie Walsh · Jane Leuchter · Jane Rawson · Jane Roberts · Jane Roberts · Jane Woollard · Janet Gilmore · Janette Ryan · Janne Støen · Jasmine Gideon · Jayne Watson · Jeannie Stirrup · Jeff Collins · Jeffrey Davies · Jenifer Logie · Jennifer Arnold · Jennifer Bernstein · Jennifer Harvey · Jennifer Petersen · Jennifer M Lee · Jenny Booth · Jenny Huth · Jenny Newton · Jenny Nicholls · Jeremy Koenig · Jeremy Morton · Jeremy Trombley · Jerry Simcock · Jes Fernie · Jess Howard-Armitage · Jesse Berrett · Jesse Coleman · Jessica Kibler · Jessica Laine · Jessica Loveland · Jessica Martin · Jessica Martin · Jethro Soutar · Jill Twist · Jim Boucherat · Jo Conlon · Jo Goodall · Jo Harding · Jo Lateu · Joanna Flower · Joanna Luloff · Joanne Badger · Joanne Marlow · Joao Pedro Bragatti Winckler · JoDee Brandon · Jodie Adams · Jodie Martire · Johanna Anderson · Johanna Eliasson · Johannes Holmqvist · Johannes Menzel · John Berube · John Carnahan · John Conway · John Coyne · John Down · John Gent · John Hodgson · John Kelly · John McKee · John Royley · John Shaw · John Steigerwald · John Winkelman · Jon Riches · Jon Talbot · Jonathan Blaney · Jonathan Huston · Jonathan Kiehlmann · Jonathan Ruppin · Jonathan Watkiss · Joseph Cooney · Joseph Hiller · Joseph Schreiber · Joshua Davis · Joy Paul · Jude Shapiro ·

Julie Gibson · Julie Greenwalt · Julie-Ann Griffiths · Julie Hutchinson · Juliet Swann · K Elkes · Kaarina Hollo · Karen Faarbaek de Andrade Lima · Karen Jones · Karen Waloschek · Kasim Husain · Kasper Haakansson · Kasper Hartmann · Kate Attwooll · Kate Gardner · Kate Griffin · Kate Mc Caughley · Katharina Liehr · Katharine Freeman · Katharine Robbins · Katherine El-Salahi · Katherine Mackinnon · Katherine Skala · Kathryn Cave · Kathryn Edwards · Kathryn Williams · Katie Brown · Katie Lewin · Katrina Thomas · Keith Walker · Kenneth Blythe · Kent McKernan · Kevin Maxwell · Khairunnisa Ibrahim · Kieron James · Kim Armstrong · Kirsten Hey · Kirsten Major · Kirsty Doole · KL Ee · Klara Rešetič · Kris Ann Trimis · Kristin Djuve · Kristina Rudinskas · Krystine Phelps · Kylé Pienaar · Lana Selby · Lander Hawes · Lara Vergnaud · Larraine Gooch · Laura Batatota · Laura Clarke · Laura Lea · Laurence Laluyaux · Laurie Sheck & Jim Peck · Lee Harbour · Leeanne Parker · Leon Frey & Natalie Winwood · Leonie Schwab · Leonie Smith · Lesley Lawn · Lesley Watters · Leslie Wines · Liam Elward · Liliana Lobato · Lindsay Brammer · Linette Arthurton Bruno · Lisa Brownstone · Lisa Dillman · Liz Clifford · Liz Ketch · Lizzie Broadbent · Lizzie Stewart · Lorna Bleach · Lottie Smith · Louise Foster · Louise Smith · Luc Verstraete · Lucia Rotheray · Lucia Whitney · Lucy Goy · Lucy Moffatt · Lucy Wheeler · Luke Williamson · Lula Belle · Lynda Graham · Lynda & Harry Edwardes-Evans · Lynn Martin · Lynne Bryan · Lysann Church · M Manfre · Madeline Teevan · Mads Pihl Rasmussen · Maeve Lambe · Maggie Humm · Maggie Redway · Mahan L Ellison & K Ashley Dickson · Margaret Briggs · Margaret Jull Costa · Maria Ahnhem Farrar · Marie Bagley · Marie Cloutier · Marie Donnelly · Marike Dokter · Marina Castledine · Marina Galanti · Marina Jones · Mario Cianci · Mario Sifuentez · Mark Dawson · Mark Sargent · Mark Sztyber · Mark Waters · Mark Whitelaw · Marlene Adkins · Martha Nicholson · Martha Stevns · Martin Brown · Martin Nathan · Martin Vosyka · Martin Whelton · Mary Carozza · Mary Heiss · Mary Wang · Mary Ellen Nagle · Matt & Owen Davies · Matt Greene · Matt O'Connor · Matthew Adamson · Matthew Armstrong · Matthew Banash · Matthew Black · Matthew Francis · Matthew Geden · Matthew Lowe · Matthew Smith · Matthew Thomas · Matthew Warshauer · Matthew Woodman · Matty Ross · Maureen Freely · Maureen Pritchard · Max Cairnduff · Max Garrone · Max Longman · Max McCabe · Meaghan Delahunt · Megan Muneeb · Megan Wittling · Meike Schwamborn · Meike Ziervogel · Melissa Beck · Melissa Quignon-Finch · Meredith Jones · Meryl Wingfield · Michael Bichko · Michael Dodd · Michael Gavin · Michael Holt · Michael Kuhn · Michael McCaughley · Michael Moran · Michael Schneiderman · Michael James Eastwood · Michelle Falkoff · Michelle Lotherington · Michelle Roberts · Mike Bittner · Mike Turner · Milo Bettocchi · Milo Waterfield · Miranda Gold · Miranda Persaud · Miriam McBride · Monika Olsen · Moray Teale · Morgan Bruce · Morgan Lyons · Myles Nolan · N Tsolak · Namita Chakrabarty · Nan Craig · Nancy Cooley · Nancy Oakes · Natalie Steer · Nathalie Atkinson · Nathan Dorr · Ned Vaught · Neferti Tadiar · Neil George · Nicholas Brown · Nick Chapman · Nick Flegel · Nick James · Nick Nelson & Rachel Eley · Nick Sidwell · Nick Twemlow · Nicola Hart · Nicola Mira · Nicola Sandiford · Nicole Matteini · Nigel Palmer · Nikolaj Ramsdal Nielsen · Nikos Lykouras · Nina Alexandersen · Nina Moore · Nina Power · Olga Alexandru · Olga Brawanska · Olga Zilberbourg · Olivia Payne · Olivia Tweed · Pamela Ritchie · Pamela Stackhouse · Patricia Appleyard · Patricia

Webbs · Patrick Cole ·
Patrick McGuinness ·
Paul Cray · Paul Daw ·
Paul Jones · Paul
Munday · Paul Myatt ·
Paul Segal · Paula
Edwards · Pavlos
Stavropoulos · Penelope
Hewett Brown · Penny
Simpson · Perlita Payne ·
Pete Stephens · Peter
McBain · Peter
McCambridge · Peter
Rowland · Peter Vilbig ·
Peter Vos · Peter Wells ·
Philip Carter · Philip
Lewis · Philip Lom ·
Philip Warren · Philipp
Jarke · Philippa Hall ·
Philippa Wentzel · Piet
Van Bockstal · PRAH
Foundation · Rachael
Williams · Rachel
Carter · Rachel
Lasserson · Rachel
Meacock · Rachel Van
Riel · Rachel Watkins ·
Rachell Burton · Rea
Cris · Rebecca Braun ·
Rebecca Carter · Rebecca
Moss · Rebecca
Rosenthal · Rhiannon
Armstrong · Rhodri
Jones · Richard Ashcroft ·
Richard Bauer · Richard
Clifford · Richard Dew ·
Richard Gwyn · Richard
Harrison · Richard
Mansell · Richard
McClelland · Richard
Priest · Richard Shea ·
Richard Soundy · Richard
Thomson · Richard John
Davis · Robert Gillett ·
Robert Hamilton · Robert
Hannah · Robin Taylor ·
Roger Newton · Roger
Salloch · Ronan
Cormacain · Rory
Dunlop · Rory
Williamson · Rosalind
May · Rosalind Ramsay ·
Rosalind Sanders ·
Rosanna Foster · Rose
Crichton · Rosemary
Gilligan · Ross Scott &
Jimmy Gilmore · Ross

Trenzinger · Rowan
Sullivan · Roxanne O'Del
Ablett · Royston Tester ·
Roz Simpson · Rozzi
Hufton · Ruchama
Johnston-Bloom · Rune
Salvesen · Rupert
Ziziros · Ryan Grossman ·
Sabrina Uswak · Sally
Baker · Sam Gordon ·
Sam Reese · Sam Stern ·
Samantha Murphy ·
Samuel Daly · Santiago
Sánchez Cordero · Sara
Goldsmith · Sara
Sherwood · Sarah
Arboleda · Sarah
Costello · Sarah
Harwood · Sarah Jacobs ·
Sarah Lucas · Sarah
Pybus · Sarah Smith ·
Sarah Watkins · Sasha
Bear · Satara Lazar · Sean
Kelly · Sean Malone ·
Sejal Shah · Seonad
Plowman · Sez Kiss · SH
Makdisi · Shannon
Knapp · Shaun
Whiteside · Shauna
Gilligan · Sheridan
Marshall · Sherman
Alexie · Shimanto · Shira
Lob · Simon Armstrong ·
Simon Clark · Simon
Harley · Simon Pitney ·
Simon Robertson · SK
Grout · Sonia McLintock ·
Sonia Pelletreau · Sophia
Wickham · Soren
Murhart · ST Dabbagh ·
Stacy Rodgers · Stefanie
May IV · Stefano Mula ·
Stephan Eggum ·
Stephanie Lacava ·
Stephen Cunliffe ·
Stephen Eisenhammer ·
Stephen Pearsall · Steve
James · Steven & Gitte
Evans · Stu Sherman ·
Stuart Wilkinson ·
Subhasree Basu · Susan
Benthall · Susan Higson ·
Susanna Fidoe · Susie
Roberson · Suzanne Lee ·
Sylvie Zannier-Betts ·
Tamara Larsen · Tamsin
Dewé · Tania Hershman ·

Taylor ffitch · Teresa
Griffiths · Terry Kurgan ·
The Mighty Douche
Softball Team · Thea
Bradbury · Therese
Oulton · Thomas Baker ·
Thomas Bell · Thomas
Chadwick · Thomas
Fritz · Thomas Mitchell ·
Thomas van den Bout ·
Tiffany Lehr · Tiffany
Stewart · Tim Hopkins ·
Tim Jones · Tim &
Pavlina Morgan · Tim
Retzloff · Tim Scott · Tim
Theroux · Timothy
Nixon · Tina Rotherham-
Winqvist · Toby Day ·
Toby Halsey · Toby Ryan ·
Tom Atkins · Tom Darby ·
Tom Dixon · Tom
Franklin · Tom Gray ·
Tom Stafford · Tom
Whatmore · Tom
Wilbey · Tony Bastow ·
Tony Messenger · Torna
Russell-Hills · Tory
Jeffay · Tracy Bauld ·
Tracy Heuring · Tracy
Lee-Newman · Tracy
Northup · Treasa De
Loughry · Trevor Wald ·
Val Challen · Valerie
Sirr · Vanessa Dodd ·
Vanessa Nolan · Veronica
Barnsley · Veronica
Baruffati · Victor
Meadowcroft · Victoria
Adams · Victoria
Huggins · Victoria
Maitland · Vijay
Pattisapu · Vikki O'Neill ·
Virginia May · Volker
Welter · Walter Smedley ·
Wendy Langridge ·
Wendy Olson · William
Dennehy · William
Schwaber · William
Schwartz · Zachary
Hope · Zack Frehlick ·
Zoe Thomas · Zoë
Brasier · Zuzana Elia

Current & Upcoming Books

RITA INDIANA is a Dominican music composer, producer and key figure in contemporary Caribbean literature; *Tentacle* won the Grand Prize of the Association of Caribbean Writers in 2017, the first Spanish-language book to do so. She is the author of two collections of stories and four novels, and is a driving force in experimental Dominican popular music with her band, Rita Indiana y los Misterios.

ACHY OBEJAS is a writer, journalist and translator. She is the author of the novels *Ruins* and *Days of Awe*, as well as three other books of fiction. She edited and translated (into English) the anthology *Havana Noir*. She currently serves as the Director of the MFA in Translation program at Mills College in Oakland, California. She is from Cuba and lives in California.

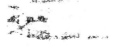

TENTACLE